ALSO BY MARISSA VANSKIKE

How It Had To Be
Bronswood

THE TURN

MARISSA VANSKIKE

This book is a work of fiction. Any references to historical events, real people, or real places are used fictitiously. Other names, characters, places, and events are products of the author's imagination, and any resemblance to actual events or places or persons living, or dead is entirely coincidental.

Copyright © 2024 by Marissa Vanskike

All rights reserved, including the right to reproduce this book or portions thereof in any form whatsoever. No part of this book may be stored in a retrieval system, or transmitted in any form or by any means, electronic, mechanical, photocopying, recording, or otherwise without express written permission of the publisher.

Cover art Mist Road in the Forest by Chang Lee/Shutterstock.com
Cover art The Bike Laying on the Asphalt by Robert_S/Shutterstock.com
Covert art Distressed Lettering by CanArtStudio/Etsy.com

ISBN: 979-8-3481-5378-6

For every reader, everywhere. The first one was for me. This one is for you.

THE TURN

THIS BOOK INCLUDES CONTENT THAT SOME READERS MAY FIND DISTRESSING. WHILE I WROTE THIS BOOK WITH CERTAIN SURPRISES IN MIND AND FEEL A BLIND READ CREATES THE MOST ENJOYABLE EXPERIENCE, IT'S NEVER WORTH THE EXPENSE OF YOUR MENTAL HEALTH. YOU KNOW YOURSELF BEST. FOR A COMPLETE LIST OF TRIGGER WARNINGS, PLEASE TURN TO THE BACK OF THE BOOK.

PROLOGUE

It serves me right for snooping around where I don't belong. I shouldn't be in this room. But then, neither should this.

Why does he have a photo of my son? Why does he have *this* photo of my son? I search the darkest corners of my mind for a reason, any reason, that could explain how this picture found its way into this bedroom. A stranger's bedroom.

I look around the room for anything else that might soothe the unbridled thoughts swirling in my head and bridge the connection I need in order to understand what I'm seeing. But nothing I concoct makes sense.

I should have kept walking, but how could I with the tiny figurine standing at attention right there, on the nightstand. Taunting me. Beckoning me to come see what else he's hiding. Was it placed there for me? Or did he make a mistake?

The temperature in the room plummets, and the photo gripped between my fingers begins to rattle in my hand. A clanging sound from the kitchen reminds me that I'm not alone. And I wasn't given permission to cross the threshold into this bedroom.

"Emily?" He calls for me. I know he's just down the hallway, preparing dinner, but his summon reverberates from somewhere that feels much farther.

"Be right there! Washing my hands!" I quickly decide that I have a minute, maybe two to look a little closer before he'll come looking for me. I slide open the drawer in the nightstand and rummage through the junk, sifting through crumpled packs of cigarettes, half eaten bags of candy, and the odd condom. Nothing to explain what I found. I'm a breath away from plunging my hand back into the drawer when a voice sounds, suddenly right behind me, startling me so badly that it's all I can do to hold onto the photo I hide behind my back as I spin to face him.

"Can I help you find something?" His voice is cool, not a hint of emotion buried underneath. It ignites every instinct within me to leave. Now.

1

EMILY
Wednesday, April 15, 2021

The coffee is percolating, the toast is toasting, the eggs are scrambling. "Harley! Get in here and have some breakfast!" I shout down the hallway towards my daughter who is, hopefully, getting dressed for school.

I turn back to the stovetop where the bacon pops. The kitchen smells heavenly and my stomach gurgles in protest at having to wait any longer to eat.

I scoop some eggs onto a plate, then pinch two pieces of bacon between cooking tongs and set them next to the eggs. The toast springs from the slots and I toss a piece on the plate. There is a sliver of space left, so I peel a banana, break half of it off to fill in the gap.

Harley shuffles into the kitchen and hangs her backpack on the back of her chair before plopping down onto one of the barstools at the island. I slide the overflowing plate across the counter as I give her a once-over. "Those aren't the clothes I laid out for you."

"Mom. I'm almost fourteen." Here comes the eye roll... "I'm perfectly capable of picking out my own clothes now." I try not to visibly cringe at the length of Harley's crop top. It doesn't show any skin until she raises her arms, after all. But, she'll inevitably raise her hand in class so what then? My thoughts run a wild course until I notice Harley's eyes fixated on her plate. "And this is way too much food for so early in the morning," she tells me.

I swallow the urge to correct Harley and subsequently endure a second teenage eye roll within a two-minute span. "We've had this discussion more often than I'm sure you'd like. But I'll remind you again—" My phone rings somewhere behind me and I ignore it. "—foods are neither good, nor bad, too much or too little. They simply nourish your body differently. Your body works really hard. Besides just growing and living each day, you also play competitive soccer. You need to feed your body, more than the average *thirteen*-year-old so it can keep working for you."

Harley sighs and I relent, just a bit. "Eat what you can, leave what you can't."

My phone rings again, so I walk over to check the caller ID. I tap the decline button and place it face down on the counter.

"Aren't you going to answer that?" Harley asks, her mouth full of eggs and toast.

I shake my head. "It's not important." I fill a cup with coffee and grab a piece of bacon, savoring the salty flavor on my tongue. I glance at the clock on the counter. We need to leave in fifteen minutes if Harley is going to make it to school on time. "Do you have everything you need for school?"

"Yup." Harley's response is curt but at least she didn't accuse me of treating her like a child again.

"We have to leave soon. Finish up and go brush your teeth."

Harley levels a stare at me and shoves her half-full plate away from her. "I'm done, anyway." She stands, bringing her plate to the other side of the island where she scrapes her uneaten food into the trash bin before loading her plate into the dishwasher.

She turns to leave, and I call out to her, "Don't forget—"

"To brush my teeth. Mom, I'm—"

"Almost fourteen years old . . . I know, I know." I pinch my lips closed as she rounds the corner and disappears down the hall where I hear the water turn on. I slip a protein bar into her backpack and wait for her to return.

The sound of the front door slamming rattles the walls. Assuming Harley must have gone straight to the car, I turn to grab my purse and check that my keys are inside. Before I turn back around, I hear the familiar thump of the newspaper being thrown away. I stopped reading the paper years ago, but I haven't gotten around to cancelling our subscription. Harley always throws them away for me, knowing I can't bear to see them anymore. I couldn't even tell you how the subscription started. Perhaps a carryover from the previous homeowners. It never seemed to matter. And once it did start to matter, it felt far easier to simply toss the papers in the trash bin. Yes, Harley's teenage years are challenging as she fights harder for her independence. But she truly is a great kid.

I turn to her. "Are you ready?"

"Yeah. I'll be in the car." Harley grabs her backpack and is out the door before I can say "alright."

My cell phone rings again and I know it's my ex, so I toss it into my purse and make my way down the foyer to the front door. I know what he wants, but I just don't have it in me to deal with him right now. I sweep past the carefully curated gallery wall, filled with an assortment of candid moments I was lucky enough to capture.

THE TURN

Most families frame their meticulously staged photos that were snapped only to the thanks of hand selected bribes unique to each child. Ours is a memorial of who we really were everyday.

I glance at the picture I sneaked when I found the kids huddled together inside of a fortress built from pillows and old sheets. Inside the fortress walls, Ryan was patiently attempting to teach his six-year-old sister, Harley, how to multiply by grouping together Skittles. Harley giggled maniacally each time she ruined his lesson by popping one into her mouth. Next to it is a photo I snapped from behind. It was Harley's first day of first grade and she was more anxious than I'd expected. Ryan asked me if he could be late to class so that he could walk Harley to hers. I couldn't say no. I fell behind them as he slung her backpack over his shoulder and wrapped his opposite arm around her. I tapped the camera button the second her head fell onto his shoulder.

The picture nearest to the front door is an action shot of Ryan during a basketball game. There was a collision between him and a player on the other team. I knew how Ryan would handle it and I snapped a picture of him as he bent over to help pick up his opponent. My hand reaches up to graze the picture of my son, just as it does every day when I leave the house. "I love you," I whisper as I open the front door and step into the morning light.

When I return home, I toss my bag into an empty chair in the living room. Taking a deep breath, I momentarily look around, feeling lost. I've never quite adjusted to the palpable silence that engulfs me when my kids aren't here. It's a different kind of quiet than when they are home but tucked away in their rooms, doing homework, or sleeping. The silence that manifests from their absence feels wrong. Usually I can ignore it, push it down and lock it away. However, Bryce's attempts at contact this morning bring the tangled mess bubbling up to the surface. At times, I'm overwhelmed with gratitude that Harley and I are still here, still together. Looking at this house we created a new life in feels miraculous in its own right. I feel strong, and happy. But most of the time, I can't escape the guilt of feeling happy again. It's a betrayal that I won't forgive myself for. Standing in this room alone is a stark reminder that while we live here, it still isn't a home. Not really.

It's time to get some work done before the clock strikes and I have to return to pick Harley up from soccer practice. I go and grab my laptop off the desk in my home office and head back to the dining room table. As a headhunter, my job affords me the flexibility to work from anywhere. My track record of successfully matching high-level candidates with executive positions has allowed me to obtain references from all over the country. It's not the most exciting job in the world, but I make a good living.

I lean back in my chair and open my email app, scanning for anything interesting. A few emails are from various human resources departments requesting updates. Several emails are from viable candidates submitting requested resumes and references.

One email catches my eye. It's out of place. The subject line reads, WE NEED TO TALK. I roll my eyes at his attempt to get my attention using all caps. The sender is my ex-husband, Bryce. I ignore my knee-jerk reaction to send the email straight to the trash folder and click the button to open it.

```
Emily, you aren't answering my calls. We need to
```

talk about Ryan. It's important. The accident was six years ago, and I need you to . . .

My mind wanders off and images flash before my eyes as I see it all again. I see the fear in Ryan's eyes when he was placed into the back of the ambulance. My heart begins to thump against my ribs. When I close my eyes, I can read the newspaper headlines that rained down on my doorstep. *Ryan Sutton Involved in Horrific Accident.* I can feel the way the town looked at me like it was my fault. My breaths become short and stunted.

I shake the thoughts from my head, hands gripped together as I wait for the flood of memories to pass, and I glance back at the email just for a moment. I know I'll have to call Bryce back. I take another minute to compose myself before I go and dig my phone out of my purse and dial his number. He probably doesn't give it a second thought that he goes on living with the same phone number he's had since he was a teenager, while I, however, had to change my number after everything that happened.

I sit back down in front of my laptop, closing the lid without bothering to read the rest of the email as the phone rings in my hand. I never could stand the way Bryce talked about Ryan's accident. Mostly because I was the only one who seemed to know the truth.

Ryan's accident wasn't an accident at all.

2

EMILY
Saturday, April 24, 2021

Trees flash on either side of the car as I lean into the turns, and I try to ignore the sweat stains my palms leave on the steering wheel. I couldn't talk Bryce into working things out over the phone, so we're going back. Back to that house. Back in time. Back to where it happened. Where everything changed.

It doesn't take long to get back to town since we didn't move that far away. Folsom felt just out of reach of everyone who knew us. Harley controls the music, using my phone to search for the songs she wants, leaving the screen inside the dashboard available to display the map guiding us to our location, not that I need it. But Harley likes to watch the blue arrow move along our route while the tiny clock in the corner tells her how much longer she'll be trapped in the car.

She picks up the phone again as we make our way down Joiner Parkway. When Harley is satisfied with the selection, a haunting cover of "Happy Together" begins to seep through the speakers. I've only ever known The Turtles to belt out the sweet lyrics to this song. But this version is far from that one. It chills me, deep in my bones.

"This is kind of spooky. You like this? You know this is a really old song, right?" I ask, my eyes not leaving the road in front of me.

Harley pretends not to hear me so I press her again. "It's older than I am . . ." I cast a quick glance out of the corner of my eye. Just enough to catch the smirk my corny joke earned.

Harley sits up a little straighter and turns towards me. "It's not spooky. It's beautiful. Just listen to it." She begins to sway back and forth in her seat with her eyes closed.

I sigh and focus on the sounds, soft and soothing, and . . . spooky. I give it my best effort and get so lost in my thoughts I don't notice that we are approaching Moore Road. My heart jolts at the realization and I quickly change into the left lane and slow down as the stop sign approaches.

I look around to ensure the roads are clear—they always are—before making an illegal U-turn.

Harley's eyes fly open at the sudden change which prompts the guide to encourage us to get back on course. "What are you doing? The map said to go straight."

I shake my head casually as if this last-minute decision is hardly worth more than a second thought. "I just decided I wanted to take a more scenic route." Harley is staring at me and I know she's not buying it. I shrug. "We're here now, so I figured we might as well see more of the town."

Harley turns back around, facing forward. "You're procrastinating. Avoiding seeing Dad."

Yes. Yes, that's easier. "You caught me."

"Speaking from experience, sometimes you just have to rip the Band-Aid off, Mom."

I snort. "You're thirteen years old. What experience are you speaking from exactly?"

The map on the dashboard reorients itself and updates the directions while Harley defends her position. "Remember last year, when Tanya stopped speaking to Laine because Laine told the boy Tanya liked that Tanya was horrible at Algebra? Well, it was totally true so Tanya brushed it off like it was no big deal. And, of course, Wills didn't care at all because he was horrible at Algebra too. Plus, he didn't even know that Tanya liked him because he's a boy and, enough said. But anyways, Tanya totally just let it fester under her skin until she exploded on me like three months later over nothing. I sat her down and she apologized and she spilled everything. She'd been holding it in all that time. I told her to just suck it up and tell Laine how she felt and that I was sure Laine didn't mean to embarrass her or hurt her feelings. Then she finally did and everything was great again."

Harley sucks in a deep breath though she actually doesn't need it. She's a fairly seasoned talker now with years of practice, despite the numerous occasions on which she's preoccupied with giving me the silent treatment.

"Wow, I didn't realize you've been dealing with so much," I reply sarcastically.

Harley ignores me and waves a nonchalant hand through the air. "It happens all the time. It's not a big deal. But my point is, just talk to Dad. Conflict resolution is all about open communication." Harley leans back against the headrest and gazes out the window. I guess her point has been made.

I can't help but smile at my daughter's innocence. I adore her for thinking our situations are so similar. For thinking that a simple discussion would fix everything. She still has so much to learn about life, and how complicated things can be. Yet, I'm amazed by how grown she seems. She's confident and sure of her opinions, I can't pinpoint when it happened. I've been so busy trying to rebuild something stable for us both that I missed the part where she blossomed into an intelligent and funny young woman.

I hate that I missed it.

My smile fades as we near The Woods, our former neighborhood, where I know Bryce is waiting for us.

3

EMILY

I shouldn't be here. I never meant to come back. It's all wrong. I don't know how to be here anymore. I look around, waiting for the familiarity to settle in, but it never comes. The only feeling that settles is dread.

This house is the same, with its cream-colored exterior and slate trim. The oil-brushed brass fixtures are exactly the way I left them. The rain chain still hangs from the gutter down to the porch. It took years of meticulous work to turn this house into a home. I stare at the canary-yellow door before me. We painted it the day we moved in. It's Harley's favorite color. Everything looks just the way it always has. Nothing has changed, yet nothing is quite the same.

I can do this. I'll simply walk inside and take care of things with Bryce, just as I always have. But my breath hitches when I reach for the doorknob. I know the risk: Opening the door will rip open the wound I've spent the last five years trying to close. I know it will never heal completely, but it bled less the longer I stayed away.

I let Harley go in first and I slam the door behind me as I step into the entryway. Something snaps at knowing he's here in the house somewhere, the anger instantly engulfing me. It's the only thing I can feel when I so much as think about Bryce.

Footsteps sound at the opposite end of the hallway. "Emily? Is that you?"

"Yes, it's me, Bryce. Were you expecting someone else? Your other girlfriend perhaps?" I lash out at him. I don't have to see his face to know that he's rolling his eyes at my jabs. Harley casts a disappointed glance over her shoulder and I tell myself to try harder.

Bryce's face sags. "Come on, Em. I thought we were past that." He glances down at Harley and seems to slip into a new skin. He was always better at pretending for Harley's sake. Bryce crouches down to hug Harley who flings herself into his arms. "Hiya, kiddo. How are you?" I notice that he doesn't have to duck down nearly as much as he did the last time he saw Harley and I wonder, again, if I've made the right decisions by her. It isn't that I'd meant to keep her from her father as much as I did. After everything that happened with Ryan, I simply needed Harley to stay close to me. In my defense, Bryce never fought me about it. It seemed that it was easier for him, and the woman he was seeing too, if he saw us less.

He lets her go and faces me. "I'm glad you came." He reaches for me but seems to think better of it, instead stuffing his hands into his pockets. A smarter choice than pulling me into his arms. A gesture I'd never be able to return. I can't even bare to look at him. I knew this wouldn't be easy, though somehow, I suddenly feel woefully unprepared for how to navigate all of this.

I step back and I watch Bryce's eyes fall to the floor before I move swiftly around him. "Well, you didn't leave me much choice, did you?"

Bryce dodges the comment and returns his focus to my daughter. I know I should give him more claim to her but it doesn't feel right, or fair. "How's soccer, Hart? I'm going to make it to a few games this year, at least. I promise." The use of her nickname pulls my attention from taking in the inside of the house, all its changes. I start to chastise him for making this promise to her for the millionth time, but his shattered promises don't seem to bother Harley anymore. She cuts me off anyway before I can get started.

"Good! I scored three goals in my game last week and coach said I can count on starting all next season." Harley still talks with her dad regularly on the phone, but seeing him in person seems to have made her forget that. She's babbling and giddy.

"That's amazing, Hart." When Harley was old enough to ask why he called her "Hart" he told her that she was his heart, and that she owned his. Bryce beams, soaking it all in. "Are you hungry? Come, let me fix you a snack."

I watch the two of them turn into the kitchen and without meaning to, I make my way back to Ryan's room. I freeze beneath the doorframe, part of me expecting my son to saunter over and wrap his arms around me. Everything is in order, as if only waiting for him to return.

Except that he won't.

He hasn't been here in nearly six long years, and he'll never be here again.

I'm lying to myself, I know, thinking this will bring me closer to him. That this will satiate my need to warp my arms around him again. To smell the top of his head and to revel in the tenor of his voice. No amount of time spent here will bring him back. It will never be enough, but even still, I just need a little longer. Here, it's just me and him, one more time.

I make my way slowly over to his dresser where a picture of him sits. It was taken the last summer I had him. He's sitting on the edge of the dock at Lake Harding, a tire swing hanging from the tree branch behind him, and he's sandwiched between his core group of friends, four young boys and two of their younger sisters tucked protectively between them.

The sticky peel of Bryce's bare feet on the hardwood floor grows louder as he approaches.

I choke down a sob, clutching the picture to my chest. "How can you sell the house?" I'd meant to scream the question at him, but I barely manage a whisper. "How can you even think about getting rid of all of his things and just . . . erasing him from our lives?"

Bryce grabs my shoulders and gently turns me around to face him. "I'm not erasing him. I could never erase our son. But I'm moving in a few weeks for work. I don't live here anymore." I hear him suck in a deep breath before he continues. "And neither do you. You haven't lived here for five years, and we can't afford to pay for a vacant house. It's time that we both try to move forward."

I can't pull my eyes away from Ryan's picture still in my hands. He looks just like his father.

Bryce turns my face up towards his. It's been years since we've really seen each other like this, but I still recognize when his eyes silently plead with me. For one fleeting moment, I want to let go of it all. The pain and the anger. But it's like no matter what I do, I just can't give it up. That rage is real and tangible. I can hold it in my hands, roll it around into a ball, and throw it back in his face whenever I want. Whenever it's all too much.

I want to hate him, too. For wanting to move on. For selling the house. For making me come back here. I know I shouldn't. That wouldn't be fair to him. He made a lot of mistakes. But, it's not his fault that his grief over Ryan couldn't touch the depth that mine did. No one's could have.

"No." I tear my face from his hand. "I'm not ready."

"You'll never be ready. I'm not ready, either!" He throws his arm out. "We can't change what happened. I wish we could, Em. You know I do." His head falls forward and I watch as it shakes back and forth, as if he's rethinking what he's about to say. "But we both deserve to try and figure out how to be happy again."

I know, deep down, that he's right, but when Ryan died, a part of me died with him. I shake my head. "I need more time."

Bryce sighs, and he stares at me as his hands rest on his hips. "Then come home. Sell your place and come back here. Give yourself a chance to mourn." When I don't say anything, he continues, "It's not like it was before. No one is talking, Em. Most of the people you were close with have moved away. There are a lot of new faces here."

The town is small, and I'm not sure I trust him. But I weigh coming back here against the consequence of saying goodbye to Ryan's things, and to this place that was just ours. That pain is unbearable.

I manage to nod my agreement and Bryce hangs his head. In relief or disappointment, I'm not sure. Either way, the house won't be his problem anymore.

He takes a step towards the door. "I'll give you a few minutes alone." Bryce leaves and gently latches the door closed behind him.

I crawl under the comforter of Ryan's bed and press his picture to my chest as my hair sweeps over the surface of his pillow where tears begin to pool. I just need a few more minutes here with my son, then I'll get up and find Bryce.

I don't have to think about it. I already know what needs to be done. We have to move back to Lincoln.

4

HARLEY

I race back to the kitchen before Dad figures out that I was eavesdropping. Parents always treat kids like we're so fragile or stupid. Like we can't possibly understand the answers to the questions we're asking. So, over the years I've learned how to be resourceful. I know how to run with light feet, and I taught myself how to muffle a sneeze so that it's silent. I can put things back exactly the way I found them, and I'm great at making just enough noise that my mom doesn't think I can hear her when she talks quietly.

Looking back, in a weird way, I think my mom would be proud of how independent I've become. She'd be proud of how well I can get through a day without needing her, or anyone else. A great pretender. She should be proud; I learned from the best.

Even when I was younger, I understood what it meant when my mom explained about Ryan's accident and how he'd died from it. My mom thinks that I don't remember Ryan. But I was eight years old when he died, and closer to nine by the time we moved away. I remember my big brother. I can recall the last few summers we spent together with our friends. I can tell her about what a great brother he was, and the ways he included me and looked out for me. I remember so much more than my mom thinks I do. But she'll never really know because she never cares to ask. So why should I care to tell?

5

EMILY
Monday, June 28, 2021

My eyes are already open when dawn slips in through the bedroom window, and I finally give up pretending to sleep. I've stopped fighting it at this point. We waited until Harley finished out the school year before moving back nearly a week ago. So, it's been nearly as long since I've slept well. Unless I decide to wildly change tactics and drown my sorrows with tequila, rum, and a choice helping of sedatives, there's not a whole lot I can do about my insomnia. Nonetheless, I promise myself I will try harder tonight, and I begin the now familiar morning trudge towards my running shoes.

I hate running. I really do. I gave it a shot a few years back when a friend suggested it as a way to clear my mind. When my head was flooded, and the dam was threatening to burst. I was desperate for release. And as much as it pains me, I have to admit that Shannon knew what she was talking about. Running saved me in more ways than one.

Before I head towards the door, I scratch out a note for Harley, just in case she wakes up and comes looking for me. She's technically a teenager now and needing me less all the time, but I can't bear the idea that she might wonder where I've gone.

I put my earbuds in, swipe open my phone, and tap shuffle on my running playlist before I can even consider looking down the hallway at Ryan's room.

When I first started running, I used the playlists that Shannon prescribed. The ones with the peppy pop jams and the latest hip-hop songs with a beat to match the thump of your shoes against the pavement. Lyrics to push you through when your legs start to scream and your mind wants to stop. But the release I needed never came. I hated all of it: every note, every word. It only stoked my rage. No one knew what I was going through, and I loathed the way all these songs asked me to be happy.

Talking with a therapist never helped either. Saying the words out loud shoved me too close to the reality I was trying to escape. But grief keeps a respectable distance when the words come from someone else, and I realized that I could sit with others' pain far better than I could my own. I craved the sting that wasn't my own.

So, one morning, as a last-ditch attempt to give running a shot, I made my own playlist filled with songs of heartache, longing, and lost love. My body responded without hesitation, having been bogged down with the ugliest of emotions for so long. On the surface, everything was fine. I still had Harley to look after. We were a team and I refused to let her down. But heartache was where I lived, and the music found me there.

Turns out, I don't need encouragement when I run. I need to feel something real. And nothing makes me feel so deeply as heartbreak. That's something I know a lot about.

As my feet pounded against the sidewalks, the ache in my muscles seemed to dull the pain in my chest and I've run every day since then, with no plans to stop.

The town hasn't changed. Lincoln, California. A small town residents refer to as "California's Paragon". I've always wondered what it was meant to be a paragon of. When we first moved here, it felt like an oasis. Like maybe it was a paragon of peace, or restoration. It's strange to think about now that it's become my own personal paragon of despair.

I make my way down the paths that trace the outskirts of town, breathing in the sweet-and-smoky scent of the oak trees. Their smell fades into a caramel aroma emanating from a row of Japanese Maple trees as I turn to run along a residential road bringing me nearer to the route I've avoided all week. A couple of miles later I turn down Seventh Street, which will lead me to Lincoln Boulevard. It's been five years since I've been down this road, but memories come flooding back to me as if it were mere days ago.

I jog past Brood Coffee, where Mrs. Baker knows you, your order, and your life history after only your first visit. I pass Bayabelle, the only boutique clothing store in town, where Ainsley can assess your size and style in a single glance. At the end of the road is the Fowler Ranch market where Mr. Candor brings in the fresh produce that he harvests himself, all the while ranting about the pesticides and chemicals big farming uses so that chain grocery stores can run honest, hardworking farmers like himself out of business with their low prices. These places, these people, were mine once. Brood was *my* coffee shop. Bayabelle was *my* favorite boutique. Fowler was *my* market. It hits me with an unwelcome weight how much I miss them. It was easier from a distance. Simple. We moved away and I missed my favorite places. Nothing more to it. But, up close, so close I can reach out and touch them, the missing draws knots in my stomach. I wonder if I'll ever feel good here again. Will they let me back in? Or has the damage done left too much wreckage behind to mend?

I blink away the thoughts as I notice just up the road is Lincoln Middle School, where Ryan met Beck, Tristan, and Charlie. The boys were so close. It was rare to see any of them without at least one of the others, if not all three. And luckily for Harley, and for me, Charlie had a younger sister. Theo and Harley became best friends, whether by chance or convenience, I'm not sure, but she was happy. We all were.

The middle school came highly recommended by the mothers around town and after a tour, I knew it was just the right place for Ryan. Harley would attend the public elementary school we were zoned for, and Ryan would go to Lincoln Middle School.

As I run past, a group of boys playing some game at a table in the schoolyard catch my eye. I wonder what they're doing at school so early in the morning, during summer break no less. I can't imagine why they'd need to be there at all, let alone at this hour. But then, as it turns out, I don't know preteen boys as well as I once thought. They appear to be taking turns swatting each other with the back of their hands, seemingly to see how much pain one can inflict, and likewise, how much pain the other can withstand.

Their bicycles lay in the grass next to them, and suddenly, the squeal of car tires and the crunch of metal against the backdrop of the morning calm are rushing towards me. My pulse quickens, and I whip my head around. But the road is empty.

I drop into a crouch and shut my eyes to steady my breathing. It's been so long since I've heard that sound that it takes nearly two minutes for the shock of it to wear off so I can finally jog home. If *home* is what I'm supposed to call it.

6

EMILY

After breakfast, Harley and I drive into town to pick up some groceries from the market. Harley has made it abundantly clear that there is nothing in the house to eat. She isn't wrong. I've managed to skirt the issue thus far by living off takeout and the food that Bryce left behind, who claimed it was rubbish to pack it all up when his daughter was moving in. But he was only eating for one. Harley had never spent any extended period of time with him, I wouldn't let her and he never asked, so he never had to learn to feed her properly. His standard for meals didn't extend far beyond boxed pancake mix and Lean Cuisine.

We step through the automatic double doors, and the world seems to tilt off balance with the weight of so many eyes flying in our direction at once.

There are some familiar faces among them, school parents, old neighbors, and sports moms. I do my best to navigate around them. I know they're wondering how I could come back after everything that happened with Ryan, and I don't blame them. They issued their judgement the first time. It was unanimous. In their eyes, I was guilty, even though the court said otherwise. It's said that time heals all wounds. But time heals nothing in a small town. It only makes things fester. Everyone always remembers.

As we stroll down the aisles, the eyes follow, and I can feel them burning my skin. Each pair is an accusation of "How could you come back? How dare you show your face here?" They follow us as we toss boxed pasta into our cart. They stare while we pick out produce. They watch as we debate Honey Bunches of Oats or Special K Red Berries cereal.

In my hurry to escape, I toss both boxes of cereal into the cart and tug Harley into a new aisle, very nearly running over Mrs. Nedley. With her neatly-pressed clothes and perfect posture, the woman could pass for a spry sixty-five years old, when I know for a fact that she has to be in her mid-eighties by now.

"I'm so sorry about that, Mrs. Nedley," I say. "I didn't see you there."

Mrs. Nedley brushes her hands down the pleats of her pants before patting the silver curls that appear to have been freshly set on her head. "No harm done, dear." When she looks up, her face pales as if she's seen a ghost. "Emily Sutton, as I live and breathe. I'd heard you were back, but I didn't believe it until just this very moment."

I would think it impossible that she's heard about my return to Lincoln, given that we've only been back for a handful of days, but word travels fast in a town like this.

"Yes, it's true. I have some personal matters to attend to." Mrs. Nedley doesn't respond, and I add, "I'm not sure how long we'll be staying." I'm not sure why I say it. I have no intention of leaving my son's room to be auctioned off to the highest bidder and then gutted to make room for some Gen Z's new home gym. But the urge to cut and run has rooted itself so strongly, I can't shake it so easily.

Mrs. Nedley looks anxious, as if a question is lodged in the back of her throat. Her eyes flicker back and forth between me and my daughter, and she opens her mouth to say something, before appearing to think better of it. Her consummate manners seem to prevail. She straightens and looks directly at Harley. "Well, dear. You don't hesitate to reach out if you need anything at all." She takes a step closer and lowers her voice to what she must think is much quieter than it actually is. "I want you to know that I never believed what they said about you. And shame on Bryce for not standing by you." She reaches out to touch Harley's cheek, and my eyes track the movement. "Such a pretty girl. You have your brother's eyes."

I pull Harley to my side. "We really should be going now."

"Of course. But Emily, don't let them get to you. Be smarter than all of them, but smart enough not to show it." Mrs. Nedley turns to go, and she calls out over her shoulder, "It's good to have you home, Emily."

Home. Is that where I am? A hand touches my arm and I turn to find Harley looking to me, silently asking for more information, but instead, I usher her to the checkout line.

We endure more glaring eyes and mouths agape as we pay for our groceries and leave the store. As soon as we are safely in the car, I blurt out, "It's going to get better. It has nothing to do with you." And before she can ask for more, I barrel out of the parking lot.

I feel guilty for the half-lie, and I can't tell if it's more for myself or for my daughter. I have no confidence at this point that it will ever get better, but there is a seed of hope nestled deep within and I grip it tight in my mind. Maybe this is my chance to finally get the answers I was denied in the haze of grief I was forced to wade

THE TURN

through all those years ago. Nevertheless, Harley seems to relax, and I can't find it in myself to care either way. Her silence is a gift, and as we drive, I think about what I want her to know. She's been doing so well these last few years, and I've worked hard to protect her from the past. From the truth.

My mind is darting from thought to thought, trying to unravel the jumbled mess tangled inside it as I pull the car to a stop in the driveway and cut the ignition. I press my thumbs into my eyes to relieve some of the pressure building in my head, groaning internally when Harley begins to swat my shoulder. "Mom!"

I turn in my seat to face her. She's looking behind me, finger pointed over my shoulder, eyes wide. My heart starts to thump widely inside my chest. I swivel in my seat and look to see what's spooked her. My breath hitches and I scramble to clamp my mouth closed trapping the scream barreling up my throat.

There. Splashed across the front of the house in red paint. I see it.

MURDERER

7

EMILY

My fingers are raw from scrubbing the paint from the door. No matter how many times I scrape my brush across the door, the shape of the letters bubbles back to the surface. Rage burns in the back of my throat, but I choke it down and dip my brush back into the bucket of stain remover. Tears blur the edges of the letters. I'm going to have to refinish the door since my brush has taken off the sealant along with the bits of red paint.

"Mom?"

The brush slips from my hand, clattering on the porch as I collapse to my knees. "Harley! You scared the sh—you scared me. What are you doing sneaking out here like that?" I blink away the tears before Harley can see them, my calm mask sliding back into place. For her sake.

"Sorry, Mom. I didn't mean to. I came around the side since you're cleaning the front door." Harley drags her foot on the ground before plopping down on the porch steps. "I didn't want you to fall inside or anything if the door swung open."

I stand up and walk over to sit with her. "It's alright. Sorry I snapped at you. I was just lost in my thoughts and didn't hear you walk up."

Harley lays her head on my shoulder, and I wrap my arm around her. "Were you thinking about who wrote that on our door?"

"It doesn't matter who did it."

"Of course it does! It was cruel. I don't understand why someone would do that to us." A tear leaks out of her eye, and I feel a damp spot bloom on my shirt sleeve.

I run a hand down her hair and over her back. "People can be that way when they're hurting."

Harley sniffles, and the sound breaks my heart. "What do *they* have to be hurt about?"

I've thought about this day for a long time. I didn't think I'd ever have to have this conversation. It's why we left. I never wanted Harley to find out. It was foolish, wishful thinking on my part. But if we hadn't had to come home, I might have been able to moderate the truth into something more manageable for Harley. It would still hurt, but she doesn't have to hurt the way I do.

I draw a long breath before answering her. "The people around here love you, and they loved your brother." My cheek drops to rest on the top of her head. "When Ryan died, the whole town was heartbroken."

Harley sits up and I see a familiar fire burning behind her eyes. It's the one that lights when she's ready to fight. She isn't prepared to accept my half-truths. Not today. "But we're the ones who lost him. He died in a car accident." She squares her shoulders at me. "Why would they write *murderer* on our door?"

I touch my thumb to her cheek. Suddenly she looks so grown,

far older than thirteen. "You were so young when he died. Your dad and I just wanted to protect you. And—" I pause, willing myself the strength to say it. "There are certain things we didn't feel you were old enough to understand then." I stand and reach out a hand for Harley. "Let's go inside."

Harley shakes her head. "No. I'm old enough to know the truth and I want you to tell me why someone painted our door."

I want to tell her no. That she's still my little girl and she always will be. But somewhere along the way, she grew up. I have to keep reminding myself of that. I shove that task in my back pocket to tend to another day. Today, I'll pretend like I already do. "I know you are. I'll tell you everything. Please?" I open the front door, leaving the brush and bucket on the porch. "Just come inside and sit down first."

I watch my daughter rise to her feet. She takes a moment to straighten her posture, and she walks, tall and assured, into the house.

I close the door softly behind me and brace myself to provide the confession my daughter has demanded of me.

The truth is, I killed my son.

8

EMILY

Against all of my raw instincts, I take a deep breath to steady myself. I stick to the facts. I tell Harley's that she's right. Ryan died in a car accident when she was eight years old. Only this time, I admit that Ryan wasn't in the car. I tell her that her brother was out riding his bike with his friends. He was too far into the middle of the road when a car, coming around the corner, struck him.

I don't tell her all of the horrible things our neighbors and so-called friends yelled at me on our way to school. I'd hate for her to have to this in her mind if we were to run into any of them when Harley starts school. I don't talk about the crazed local media frenzy that erupted in the wake of his passing. I don't tell her about the reporters that waited to ambush us outside our house, and I don't tell her how we'd had to turn up her sound machine to drown out the noise from the people who pounded on our front door in the middle of the night. Those memories are too close, and I don't think I'll survive them a second time.

Instead, I tell her about the trial to determine the fate of the driver, and I exert all my effort to point my words towards the affection of a town that loved Ryan enough to avenge his death. When my voice breaks, I close my eyes and clench my fists tighter, so my hands won't shake.

I give her a moment to weigh all this new information before telling her the final truth. The one that I fear will rip her away from me.

I explain that the reason someone painted that hideous word on our door is because I was driving the car that killed Ryan. I tell her it was an accident. The worst kind of accident, and that the court agreed, exonerating me.

I stop when I see tears in Harley's eyes, as much for my own sake as for hers. I'm not sure how much longer I can hold myself together, even for her. I gave Harley everything I thought she could handle. The truth. Not the whole truth, but I remind myself that I'm not under oath. Not anymore.

I hold my breath as I wait for my daughter's reaction. And for her judgement.

Harley stands and takes a step towards her bedroom, and I feel myself begin to splinter. She takes another step before she changes her mind. I hear her exhale loudly as she spins on her heel and marches over to me. Her face is different. Determined and steady, she wraps her arms around me and buries her face in the soft spot just inside my shoulder. Despite my insurmountable guilt, I hold her close.

A tiny sound escapes her lips and she whispers, "It's going to be okay, Mom. We'll be okay." The words land softly in my ear, and one part of my heart manages to stitch itself back together, while another piece fractures further.

THE TURN

By the time I send Harley to bed, my body is weak with exhaustion. I creep into Ryan's room and without turning on a light, I walk straight to his bed to crawl beneath his blanket. It's been nearly six years, and I can tell from the scent that the bedding has been washed recently. Bryce probably cleaned it before we came, thinking he'd avert a meltdown. Regardless, I swear I can still detect the faint scent of Ryan's shampoo on the pillow and his deodorant on the edge of the comforter. I inhale deeply, taking in the woodsy aroma with a hint of leather that Ryan loved, and close my eyes, remembering before. I let myself live there for a moment. After some time, perhaps just minutes, sleep offers to take me, and I surrender.

9

HARLEY

I'm not sure what my mom meant when she said the whole thing with Mrs. Nedley at the grocery store had nothing to do with me. Maybe she could tell I was on edge. I know all about Dad's affair since Mom wasn't exactly quiet about it. But, I had no idea that people said such horrible things about my mom when Ryan died. How screwed up is that?

But it wasn't Mrs. Nedley making me feel so uncomfortable. Except for the whole touching my face thing. That was cringe. She clearly knew me, but I don't know her and I'm not sure why she felt entitled to touch me. Mom has never tolerated stuff like that though, and when she stepped in, it was a relief. She's always bending over backwards to make everything seem like it's not a big deal. Like, there's never anything for me to worry about. And that's the part that worries me the most.

I know more than my parents ever thought I did, but I always kept it to myself because it was easier that way. As time went by, Mom finally started to seem happy again and I didn't want to hurt her by asking for the truth. But the paint on the door changed everything and I can't ignore it. I wanted to let it go, for Mom's sake. She'd prefer it, I know, but spending all these years without my brother only to find out she's been lying about what happened to him . . . I've always knows there's more, and now it's really starting to piss me off. It feels like in order to hide the bad thing that happened to him, we have to hide the good things too and I'm sick of living with only half of my brother's memory.

I thought I finally got through to her when I demanded answers just now. I wanted to hear it from her. I wanted her side of the story. But she obviously wasn't ready to tell me. I don't think she'll ever be ready to tell me. She was just feeling cornered when someone called her a "murderer" in front of the entire neighborhood.

Mom told me how the town was hurting because they loved Ryan and me. But I already knew that. Ryan was a different kind of twelve-year-old boy. He was always out to help people. He was often late coming to the car after school because he was helping Ms. Canton put the art classroom back in order. If a customer at Brood wasn't paying attention, he would hand deliver their drinks to them. He always helped old Mr. Shefield, who lived next door, carry his groceries inside. Even though he'd play along with his friends' silly games in the summertime, Ryan always gave back the things he won from them.

Mom admitted she and Dad had kept a lot from me before. But she's still hiding things. I know because she left out parts that I remember as clear as day.

I was young, sure, but not so young that I forgot about the people who yelled at Mom all the time, or the cameras that camped out on the front lawn. Or the way Mom and Dad used to put a jacket over my face when we came out of the house, though they never told me why I had to hide. I wasn't so young that when the parents got together and told us to go play in our rooms, Theo and I wouldn't sneak around to eavesdrop because it was the only way we could find out what was really going on.

    I knew something bad had happened. Something bigger than an accident. But until now, Mom kept it to herself. Or at least she thinks she did. I know she thinks she's still protecting me, but she needs protection too sometimes. She can keep her secrets, for now. It's not like I haven't kept a few of my own. But she never asks. No one asks. No one asked me if I wanted to move back here. No one asked how I feel being dragged back to this town and back to the secrets I haven't thought about keeping in years. The one I keep for Ryan. The one I'll keep on keeping because he asked me to. Does it even matter anymore? I hate that he isn't here to tell me.

10

EMILY
Tuesday, July 20, 2021

We walk into the indoor arena for Harley's soccer lesson. She began playing competitively three years ago. It didn't come easily for her at first, but she loved it. Harley has never shied away from a challenge and the more she played, the better she got. One day, about a year after she'd started, everything about the sport looked like it clicked into place. I'd never seen her happier than when she was on the field with her team. Just four months ago, her coach told me that if she improved her speed and agility, she could potentially move up to the next age bracket early, though she'd be the youngest player on the team. Harley stood next to me for that discussion and I watched as her eyes glazed over. At the time, I wasn't sure if she was hesitant because she was nervous about playing with older girls, but when we got home and the new information had set in, Harley practically begged me. She was locked in and after everything that she's been through in the last six years, I couldn't refuse her.

But that was before. Before we were dragged back here. It's

been a few weeks since we moved back. Harley got a bit lost in the midst of everything that was happening after Ryan's death. I hadn't meant to lose her. God knows that in reality, the only thing I wanted was to protect her. It was my only focus. Looking back with clear eyes, I see all the ways I stopped seeing Harley and only saw what I needed to do in order to push the pain down. I know Harley feels forgotten. She hasn't said as much but she was a literal part of me, and I know her better than anyone. I can't bear the thought of her feeling neglected again, so I called the first speed and agility coach I could find.

We step onto the turf where a man stands waiting with a girl who looks to be about Harley's age. He looks up and walks across the field towards us, one hand extended.

He stops in his tracks just a couple steps away. "Em? Emily Wilks . . . is that you?"

We were so young the last time I saw him, just coming into our own. He's a decade or so older now, with a few handfuls of tattoos lining his arms, but I still know his face. "Sawyer? Sawyer Dennis from down the street?" I reach out to take his hand but his eyes crinkle in the corners and he careens forward faster than I can register, wrapping me in a hug.

"I can't believe it's you!" As if remembering why we are here, he glances at my daughter. "You must be Harley." Harley nods and glances my way. It always takes her some time to open up to someone new. Sawyer looks up at me and my bottom lip falls open.

From a distance, it wasn't readily apparent how beautiful he's become, with his tanned skin, and his dark hair cut short and swept cleanly to one side. His cheekbones are chiseled to a devastating sharpness. I can't remember the last time I've even noticed a man this way and I zip my lips back together, embarrassment radiating through me. I'm in no position to be thinking about Sawyer like this. Or anyone, for that matter.

I bob my head in Harley's direction. "Yes, this is Harley and it's Emily Sutton now. She . . ." His eyes dart down to my hand which no longer has a ring on it, and I realize I'm on the verge of vomiting an explanation that he didn't ask for and I sputter to a stop. Of course, now I've started a sentence that I'm taking too long to complete. "She loves soccer," I spit out just before nearly drowning in my own stupidity. I've never been so tongue tied around a man in my life, but then I always did have a crush on Sawyer, even when we were kids. I'm too old to feel this nervous talking to a boy. It's middle school all over again. "Sorry, I just wasn't expecting you. I think the coach I was talking to on the phone was Stephen?"

Sawyer grins, looking me right in the eyes as he speaks. "Yeah, sorry about that. Coach Ambrose had a scheduling conflict, so I offered to fill in for him. It's nice to meet you, Harley. Follow me." He spins to make his way back over to the girl he left on the side of the field and we trail behind him. "Raina, this is Harley." He pulls the girl closer to him as he shifts his attention to my daughter. "Harley, this is my daughter, Raina. I've been coaching her for nine years. It's in Stephen's notes that you're new in town, so I thought maybe you'd like to meet someone your age who you might be playing with." I watch the girls size each other up, but in a friendly way. A moment passes before I realize Sawyer is talking to me again. "I can't believe we both wound up just a couple towns over from where we grew up."

I watch as Harley pinches her eyebrows together and looks at Sawyer. "We're not new here. We—"

I can't get into this right now. "We used to live in the area," I explain, cutting Harley off, "but that was years ago. We only recently came back."

If Sawyer is confused, he hides it well. "Well, welcome back then." He tips his head in my direction.

"And we may scale back the extra lessons when school starts. I'm not sure yet."

Harley glares at me. "Mom . . ."

I resist rolling my eyes at her attitude. "School is a priority, and soccer takes up most of your free time as is." I look at Sawyer. "I just want to make sure she's not falling behind in school."

His eyes soften as he smiles at me. "Of course. I understand." He turns to the girls. "Should we get started? Raina, will you take Harley through the warm-up?"

The girls set their water bottles down and Raina grabs Harley by the hand, dragging her excitedly over to the far side of the field where they begin to jog. Raina is skipping more than she is jogging, looking animatedly back and forth between Harley and the turf in front of her.

I look back over at Sawyer who is leaning in towards me lowering his voice. "I think Raina is excited to have a new friend to do extra practices with. She's a bit obsessed with the sport." His eyes are deep chestnut, but they sparkle in the same way the sunlight dances along the tiny peaks dotting the ocean's surface. "I hope you don't mind that I brought her along. I know this is a private session. I just thought it could be helpful this first time in making Harley feel more comfortable."

I smile and shake my head. "No, I don't mind. It could be good for Harley. We could be here for a while."

Sawyer nods. "It's really good to see you. We should catch up some time." He breaks his gaze and pops a whistle into his mouth, letting out a sharp chirp. "Ladies! Less chatting, more stretching . . . Raina, I'm talking to you!"

I squeeze my lips together to stifle the laugh that bubbles up at the sight of his daughter's dramatic eye roll, the universal language of preteen girls, and I catch Sawyer glance at me in my peripheral. Maybe this could be good for both of us.

11

EMILY
Thursday, July 22, 2021

I need to get back to work. I stare at the stack of applications in front of me. My current clients understood when I requested two weeks' time to move and adjust to our new life, but they still have job vacancies to be filled. After taking an extra week, I know that if I don't jump back in sooner rather than later, they may seek another contractor.

The stack of resumes in front of me is nearly three inches tall and after thirty minutes of reading the same sets of statistics, the applicants have begun to bleed together, none of them standing apart from another.

After some time away, I've been thinking more about finding a new career. Headhunting isn't particularly satisfying, but it's difficult to argue with the ability to be available for whatever Harley needs. Maybe something with a similar skill set. I am gifted in the professional matchmaking department. Perhaps that skill would translate to some other kind of matchmaking. Romance? Not that

THE TURN   53

I'm in any way qualified to give people advice on dating seeing as I have been single for the last five years, and married to Bryce for nearly fifteen years before that. But those who can't do, teach. Or so they say. I find my thoughts homing in on Sawyer without permission. To say he was a surprise doesn't quite cover it. Despite how badly I embarrassed myself in front of him, I can't deny that the flirtatious spark that came alive was actually fun. He was a natural on the field, and his confidence only makes him more attractive. I wonder what skills he might have off the field . . . Dear lord. I can't believe I just went there. I ought to go stick my head in the freezer until I cool off.

While I'm able to reign my thoughts back from the wildly inappropriate, my mind continues to drift away from my work and after nearly an hour I find myself thinking about Zola and Annalee.

The three of us had young boys, all around nine years old when we met, and Zola and I also had daughters the same age. When Zola moved to Lincoln eight years ago with three children in tow, our boys became inseparable. Once our boys brought Tristan into the fold, after meeting him in the school yard, Ryan, Beck, Charlie, and Tristan were rarely seen separately. And every summer, when school was out, we'd spend six weeks all together at Zola's cabin in Lake Harding. Harley would stay in a bedroom with Zola's daughter, Theo. The boys would usually camp out in the main room so that they could all stay together. Annalee would usually slip back to her own cottage that she'd inherited from her parents a short way up the road and return at breakfast the following morning. As it turns out, many of Lincoln's residents escape to Lake Harding when they need a break. At just an hour and a half away, the gorgeously maintained slice of nature sits just next to the Truckee border, making it an easy and perfect family getaway. It's not uncommon for Lincoln residents to own one of the adorable cottages, as they are often passed down from generations before who have since migrated into town. Several of them rent their cottages out the rest of the year and make a decent stream of income this way. Or so Annalee told us when she began renting her cottage out to vacationers years ago.

It's been far too long since I've spoken to either of my closest friends. I'm not even sure if they still live in Lincoln. That's how removed I made myself. They may have new phone numbers too. They may want nothing to do with me after what I did. Before I can talk myself out of it, I grab my cell and dial Zola's number. She picks up on the third ring.

"Hello?" Zola's voice is a salve. Her greeting is like a fresh bite of disinfectant on an old wound long ignored, followed quickly by the soothing remedy of a familiar friend. Guilt burns the back of my throat at the time I let pass without her.

"Zola? It's me . . . Emily."

"Emily! God, how are you?" Zola pauses, but not long enough to let me respond. "And where the hell have you been?"

I don't know what to say. I didn't have anything prepared. "I'm sorry. I know I've been a shitty friend."

"A shitty friend? Em, you basically disappeared on us! We tried calling over and over. We came to the house and one day, you were just . . . gone. We tried so hard, but you pushed us away, Em. We could have been there for you. We *wanted* to be. But you didn't tell me or Annalee where you went and when we asked Bryce, he just told us to give you some space. He always was an asshole . . ."

A sour huff escapes my lips. "Yeah. Well, I didn't really give him any say in any of it." I hate myself just a little bit for giving him that credit, even though he isn't here to bask in it.

Zola sighs on the other end of the phone. "Emily, are you alright?"

"Yeah, I'm fine," I say because it's what I always say. It's a reflex now and I sound too chipper. I'm tempted to leave it there, but I'm tired of carrying the weight of the last six years around with me. "Actually, no, not really. But I want to be. I'm trying." I quickly change the subject. "How are you? How are the kids?"

I can almost picture Zola rolling her eyes at me. Even at my best, I was never any good at talking about myself. "Mostly good. Beck is counting down the days to graduation. He got into UC Davis, pre-med, so he won't be too far away from home." I smile. Beck was always a brilliant kid, quietly learning about the way this muscle contracted, and the way some element mixed with some other molecule would create some specific kind of compound. "Theo has discovered that she likes to dance. Ballet, mainly. Who knew her love of tutus wasn't just a phase?"

Zola chuckles lightly but stops there. I know she probably doesn't want to talk about him, but I need to know. "How is Charlie doing?"

Charlie was the one we all worried most about. Between the trauma he endured from the people who were entrusted to care for him, and what happened with his mother back at Bronswood, he was surprisingly resilient. I know Zola was worried he wouldn't have a normal life again, that it would be too much to truly come back from. But, he was thriving in Lincoln with his sister, and Beck, and his new friends. Something in Charlie snapped when Ryan died though, and it was like we lost him too.

"I don't know, to be honest, Em." Zola's tone softens. "He still has good days, and bad. But he seems to be making strides since his grandma took him to live with her in Truckee. The quiet life out in nature seems to be good for him. Plus, he's done a lot of therapy and their dad has been shockingly reliable when it comes to checking in and visiting with Charlie and Theo."

I nod, though Zola can't see me. "I miss him."

"I miss him, too."

"I miss you all. Have you talked to Annalee lately?"

"Yeah, your being MIA aside, not too much else has changed. We talk all the time. And we still do the summer vacations together. You should call her though. I know she'd love to hear from you too."

"I think I will," I reply, knowing that I don't mean it. Then again, I never thought I'd call Zola again. So maybe I could mean it, one day. "I'm back in Lincoln."

"What? You are? How? Why? Say more."

"Bryce said he was selling the house, so I didn't have much of a choice." I can't stop the resentment that seeps into my voice.

"I'm so sorry, Em. What can I do?"

Really, what could she do? There's nothing to be done at this point. I say as much. The silence is sticky, and it takes a moment to scrape off the self-consciousness I've never felt with Zola before. I clumsily tell her about Harley and her blossoming soccer passion, and how I became a sought-after headhunter when, as a secretary, my former boss who had a long list of personal affronts, jokingly tossed me a slush pile of resumes and dared me to find one gem in the rubble that he missed. I found him eight, left them in a pile on his desk, along with my letter of resignation. When I contacted the candidates two weeks later and discovered, to no one's surprise, that they'd yet to be contacted by my former company, I offered to put them in touch with a new firm that came highly recommended by theirs truly. We manage to stumble through another twenty minutes of conversation before she needs get back to her life. The one I'm not a part of anymore. But maybe I could be again. I hope so. I'm not sure how long I'll last here on my own.

"Listen," Zola says, "I've got to run, but I'd love to see you. Can we meet soon?"

"I'd like that," I say, and it feels like I'm telling the truth. I think I'd like that very much.

"Great, I'll text you at this number? And call Annalee! Do it before I tell her we talked. You know how she hates to be the last to know."

I chuckle. It's classic Annalee to feel like she's kept out of the loop. There's only the three of us. The loop is really a triangle and someone has to be last. "I will. Talk to you soon."

"Bye, Em."

I hang up the phone and consider whether I should call Annalee. Zola was always the more understanding, the least judgmental of the three of us. I knew Zola would forgive me, but I expected to work harder for it. It's not the last hard conversation I need to have with Zola, though it's an unexpected relief to have this first step behind me. I didn't expect to feel so unburdened after talking to Zola, but I can't deny that I feel a certain sense of support that I've never admitted to needing. Calling Annalee after years of avoidance would be asking for more than an earful. I decide to save that for later and I fall back on the sofa, tossing my cell phone off to the side.

I sit for a minute with my eyes closed. When I open them, the stack of work on the coffee table is still there, but I stand up and walk to Ryan's room.

12

EMILY

As I make my way down the hall, I pass the closet where we stored our overflow. Stuff like blankets, bedding, board games, toiletries. Things that would make a guest feel more comfortable or ensure that our own were always cozy enough.

My hand grazes the knob on the door as I glide past, and I wonder at the way I stopped measuring time in firsts after Ryan died. How instead, I began to measure in lasts.

When was the last time I absentmindedly pressed this closet door until the latch clicked in place after Ryan pulled a blanket down from the shelf but left the door cracked open? Not open enough to be accused of not having closed it, but just enough that he hadn't quite done the job. When was the last time that I tucked Ryan in, or read him a story before bedtime? When was the last time I had to ask him to clear his plate from the table after dinner?

It's painful to know I'll never again be given the chance to revel in these mundane things that would normally be cause for complaint. It's even more cruel that I can't remember the last time I'd done any of it.

I continue padding down to the end of the hallway and I push open the door to Ryan's room.

The air inside is stuffy and warm. I walk to the opposite wall, draw back his curtains, and slide the window open. I suck in a mouthful of the fresh, albeit hot and tacky, air coming in from outside before turning back to face his room.

All of Ryan's things are still here. I glance over at the photo from Lake Harding that I held in my hands months ago. It sits next to a small table lamp with a base made from driftwood. Ryan picked it out himself because it reminded him of summers at Zola's cottage. A thin sheen of dust has settled on the dresser's surface that I hadn't noticed when I crawled into his bed three weeks ago, and I drag my finger lazily through it, trying not to be angry with my ex-husband for stripping Ryan's bedding of his scent while letting the rest of his room become so filthy.

My son was never a big hoarder of things, unlike Harley who seemed to clutch every broken barbie limb, dried-up marker, and scrap of paper as if they were lifelines. Ryan had very few things he treasured enough to keep for any length of time. Only a handful of photos were deemed worthy of frames and put on display around his room. A couple of trophies from the years he spent playing basketball with Beck, Charlie, and Tristan. A few trinkets he'd collected from his friends during the summer. They would make up games together and the winners were gifted a special item from each of the losers. Sometimes the treasures could be earned back by completing a dare or some other task or chore dished out by the holder of the item. I never could quite keep up with their rules.

Ryan's favorite summer was when the boys were around ten

years old. That was the summer that Ryan dared Charlie to be the first to test out the new tire swing that hung from a tree branch that jutted out high over the lake. Charlie put on a brave face, but in the end, he couldn't let go of the swing. The cost of his failure to complete the dare was a tiny Hulk Lego figure. My heart broke for him. I knew how special that Lego was to Charlie. I planned to make Ryan return it, but later that night, I went to knock on their bedroom door and I overheard Ryan telling Charlie that it was his favorite prize and how he promised to always keep it safe. Charlie had seemed at peace about the whole thing, and they were off to play new games the next morning.

Later that week, Ryan went on to collect Beck's most cherished baseball, signed by Pablo Sandoval, a few trinkets I didn't recognize like the odd poker chip or a pair of pilot's wings that belong on a lapel, and Tristan's new Canon Rebel, a ridiculously expensive camera for a teenage boy. But Tristan was very artistic, and his dad felt that if Tristan had great things, then Tristan wouldn't mind his absence. I was quite upset at the boys' casual disregard for such an expensive item and argued that ten-year-olds should not be allowed to make those kinds of choices. Annalee, on the other hand, was unruffled and insisted rules were rules. If Tristan wanted to give away his beloved camera, that was his decision, and he would have to learn how to live with it if he regretted it later. She called it a valuable life lesson though I always suspected she'd have been all too thrilled to inform her ex-husband that the camera had been destroyed. Either way, over the next couple years, the kids got a lot of use out of it documenting their time together.

Ryan never lost these items in the following summers. The couple summers he had left. Partially because he never risked them in any more of the boys' games, and partially because he rarely

THE TURN

accepted a challenge he knew he couldn't complete. But for Ryan, it was never about the competition. It was about the prize itself, a piece of the people who meant the most to him that he could hold on to. He cherished them.

Ryan saved the items together in a navy-blue box kept inside the storage drawer beneath his bed. Right next to his most precious possession: a miniature Boeing B028 Superfortress model airplane that he built when he was six with his dad. It had a wonky left wing and a missing propeller after being played with and subsequently glued back together, but Ryan refused to get rid of it. As he grew older, it became something he displayed, and eventually, put away when he caught Harley flying it around his room.

I kneel beside the bed and push the comforter back to open the drawer. I look inside, but the box that I came for is missing. I swipe a hand around to see if the box had slid to the back, but I find nothing. Bryce must have moved it somewhere. Why would he do that? Damn it, Bryce. He better not have taken it with him.

I put the bed back the way I found it and pull my phone out to make a note to ask Bryce where Ryan's box is before making my way back to the living room. I close the door behind me, remembering how stale the room was when I walked in.

I should leave the door open more often, but I hadn't been ready before. And I'm not ready today.

13

HARLEY

I press my door closed as quietly as possible. Mom was talking to Zola on the phone while I was eating breakfast in the kitchen, but when she moved into Ryan's room, curiosity got the best of me and I crept up to the door. She was riffling through a drawer beneath his bed. I thought about going in, to see if I could help her with whatever it was that she was looking for, but it felt like a private moment, so I slipped back into my room.

    I could only hear one side of the conversation, but hearing Zola's and Theo's names again made my heart hurt. After we moved, we never talked about them anymore. Mom never mentioned their names, never called her or Annalee. It wasn't fair. She probably thought I would just forget all of them as time went on, just like she thought I forgot about everything else.

    But how could I forget Theo? She was my best friend. We were just kids so we were kind of friends with everyone, but Theo was different. She was the sister I never had. Not that Ryan wasn't enough for me, but he was older, and he was a boy. I wanted someone who I could play makeup with, who liked pastels, and would daydream about being a princess with me. My mom thought I'd forget about Theo, but really it was my mom who forgot about me.

It's nearly ten thirty in the morning so I change out of my pajamas and toss the hoodie I slept in, since Mom's been overcompensating with the air conditioning lately, onto the back of my desk chair, or at least, in the direction of the chair. I hear a light smacking of fabric on the floor, but I don't bother to check whether the sweatshirt made it to its destination. It's probably close enough.

In the closet are several boxes still waiting to be unpacked. I slide one out and peel back the flaps. Mom would flip if she saw the way I packed. I admit this one looks more like someone's junk drawer vomited into a cardboard box. What mom never understood is that there's a system. It's chaos to her, but I know exactly where everything is, which is how I knew to pull out this particular box.

After some light digging, I find what I'm looking for wrapped in an old T-shirt for safe keeping. I can't say why it mattered so much at the time since the contents within have seen better days. I gently unfold the shirt and pull out the model airplane. Ryan knew how much I loved to play with it. He finally decided that I needed it more than he did. Mom never knew he gave it to me, and I never told her. I was afraid she'd make me give it back. I only played with it when I knew Mom was busy, then I'd slip it back into the corner of my closet until the next time.

I pull open the rear ramp of the plane and gently pull out the paper hidden inside the body. I unroll the tiny stack of photos and pluck the one from the top, setting the others to the side. This picture somehow feels both like it was taken so long ago and like it was just the other day. I run my fingers over the faces that gaze back at me.

It's my favorite photo from that last summer. Parents only like to keep the photos they think look the best. The ones where they make kids pose this way, and wrap this arm around that shoulder, and smile with your teeth showing, and cross those legs, hold hands. They never choose the real pictures. They never really see us.

That's why I keep this picture when Mom printed several handfuls for possible framing. We're all out by the dock at Zola's cabin. Theo and I are huddled together and she's giggling about something I'm whispering in her ear. Ryan is looking away from the camera and his hand is messing up Charlie's hair. Tristan and Beck are wrestling in the background. And behind us, you can see the new tire swing hanging from the tree branch. This picture is real. We're all there. All seven of us.

14

EMILY
Tuesday, July 27, 2021

I spy Annalee and Zola seated at a small table by the windows. The bell over the door of Rebel Hen chimes as I step through, and the air seems to have been sucked from the room as all eyes look up at me. The cafe is new since I left Lincoln. That this is the place Zola and Annalee chose to meet, rather than the comfort of my favorite coffee house, Brood, is another reminder of the way life moved forward for everyone else here, despite the fact that for me, life here had ended. I duck my head and make my way to where Zola is standing, her arms outstretched.

The three of us exchange greetings and I take a seat by the window facing into the cafe. An older couple sits across the way, next to a small fireplace, reading a copy of the *Lincoln News Messenger*. The old man's eyes glance at me from over the top of his paper and then back to the article clutched in his hands.

The cafe is filled with the smell of ground coffee beans and the warm, fruity aroma of freshly baked pastries. On the other side of the room is a small nook, where a group of women sit, casually feeding their babies as they chat. One of the women stares openly at me while another tosses covert looks over her shoulder, which she tries to mask by raking her chin across her T-shirt. I turn my attention to my friends with an awkward, rueful smile tugging at the corners of my mouth. "Thank you for meeting me. I owe you both an apology."

Zola waves my comment away and sets her mug down. She'd mentioned not much has changed and I'd be willing to bet that her mug is filled with a peach pie latte. "You don't owe us anything. You were dealing with a lot. Too much, really." She pushes an untouched glass of ice water and a small mug of black coffee towards me and I take a grateful sip. The liquid is hotter than I anticipated, making me flinch when it sears my tongue. "Though, now that you're here, I wouldn't turn away an explanation."

Annalee takes a gulp from her own cup and watches me. She hasn't said a word. Zola might not need my apology, but Annalee specializes in grudges. There is no grey area when it comes to her. She's fiercely loyal, but with that comes a strong reaction to perceived betrayal. I turn my body to face her as I reach a hand across the table. "I am so sorry. For everything. I'm sorry I just left the way I did. I'm sorry for not taking your calls. I wasn't the only one who lost Ryan. You and the boys did too. I was just trying to survive everything that happened. I have a lot of regret about the way I handled things." I drag my eyes up to meet theirs. "I know. I don't know how to make it right, but I want to try. I was drowning, and it felt like no one noticed. And then the whole trial . . ." I fold my tongue on itself inside my mouth, running it back and forth feeling the fuzzy texture the coffee burn left while I wait for Annalee to say something. Watching her is like being lured in by a predator with a beautiful light on its head hiding the rows of razor-sharp teeth just behind it. I've offered myself over to her. Now I wait for her bite.

Annalee seems to chew on my words and she pushes a strand of dark brown hair behind her ear before replying with a half shrug, throwing away my explanation. I look to Zola for some help and though her eyes are soft, she simply pushes the corner of her mouth up into a half smirk, clearly trying not to enjoy this too much. She offers an olive branch, talking about Annalee as if she isn't seated right next to me. "Don't be too hard on her. She was worried sick about you for years."

I shake my head and let my eyes fall to the tabletop. Shame radiates through my body. So many years, wasted. Years that I could have leaned on my friends. Time that we could have spent helping each other heal. Instead, I ran. I pretended as though none of it was happening and that we'd be fine on our own, just Harley and me. We didn't need anyone's pity.

Maybe if I had stayed, things would have been different. Maybe we would have made it through, come out stronger or more unified somehow. Or maybe the town would have destroyed what was left of me.

The old man seated behind Zola, continues to watch me, the edge of his paper curled back over his hand. He doesn't even have the decency to avert his eyes when I catch him. "No one was listening to me. No one wanted to hear me," I say as I swirl the water in my glass around with my straw. "I know what I saw that day and . . ." I'm having trouble explaining, and this man won't stop staring at me. "I thought I could come back here now and start again. But it's dredging up so much . . . I don't know. I have no idea how to do this. How to be here."

Zola stops my hand with hers. "We believe you. You don't

have to get into this again so soon. We *know* that you didn't hit Ryan with your car on purpose." The old man leans in toward his wife, shaking his head, and I can hear him tutting his disapproval.

"Of course I didn't. But I wasn't the only one there that day."

Annalee finally speaks up. "No, you weren't. All our boys were there and they testified, as witnesses. Which was incredibly traumatic for them."

My blood is beginning to boil now. "Yes! Them, plus the other boy. The one who didn't show up. The boy who pushed my son into the road!" My voice has drawn the attention of every person in the cafe.

Annalee stops me with a single, blunt word. "Alright."

"Alright?" I know Annalee wears a tough shell around her. But that was curt even for her.

Annalee shrugs. "Alright. You apologized. I accept your apology."

"Then why doesn't it feel like you do?"

Annalee sighs and leans in. "Emily, we love you. You have endured the most painful thing a mother could ever endure. But, there was no other boy." She reaches across the table for my hand and I look her in the eyes. She must have rethought her choice of words because she looks to Zola for backup before quickly adding, "Everyone deals with grief differently, Em. You were the only one who saw him that day and the description you gave didn't match anyone our boys could identify."

Our boys. She said it like they belong to all of us, the way they once did. But they aren't mine anymore. They belong to Annalee and Zola. I can't go through this again. I can't have this argument with them right now. Besides, time has made everything a little hazy. I'd once been so sure about all of it. I could see the foot jut out with shocking clarity. But everything happened so fast. The fifth boy wasn't one I knew. Dark curls on top of a face that I didn't recognize. Eyes too far away to betray their color. As soon as I had Ryan in my arms, that boy was gone and everything else melted away too. The next thing I remember with any kind of surety, was being picked up off the hospital floor.

I lean back in my chair and press my thumbs into my eyes. I fold my hands into my lap, exhausted, already needing a distraction from this conversation. "I don't want to fight. I'm sorry. I'm just a little scattered right now. Bryce is being a complete ass and I'm trying to help Harley adjust to a new life and a new soccer coach, and I need to get back to work or my clients may drop me. It's just been overwhelming."

"Of course it is. I can't imagine," Zola says.

"What is going on with Bryce?" Annalee asks. "He must know you're back."

"Yeah, he knows. He's the reason I'm here." I sigh. "He wanted to sell the house and clean out Ryan's room. He said I wasn't living there, and neither was he for much longer, so it didn't make sense to keep paying the mortgage."

Annalee nods, no doubt thinking how practical that sounds.

"I couldn't stand the thought of my last ties to him being severed, so I moved back." I pause, unsure of how much more I want to say about it right now. "Then, I was in Ryan's room and looking for something of his. This box he had, but it wasn't where Ryan always kept it. I called to ask Bryce where it was and he swears he doesn't know. He's just being a dick because I won't forgive him for what he did." I take a gulp from my water glass. "Enough about Bryce. I just wanted to see you both and, you know, catch up. How are the boys?"

I listen to Annalee tell me about Tristan and how he'd aced all of his classes, particularly art, while tackling being the star running back on the varsity football team at Lincoln High School this past year. Charlie is still doing well, no major update since my phone call with Zola the prior week. Though she's happy to share more about Beck thriving in his science classes, chemistry in particular. He's doing so well, in fact, that he's been taking a couple of advanced courses this summer at a local junior college and preparing for his senior year.

My heart warms at the thought of the boys doing so well. I wish I could have been there to watch them grow, knowing full well that it would have been extremely painful without Ryan by their side. "I am so glad they're doing well. I really would love to see them. Maybe we could get together? I know Harley would love to see Theo, too."

Zola nods. "Definitely! Theo would be thrilled." I glance down at my phone and tell them I need to get going so that I can run before Harley's soccer lesson this afternoon.

A snort comes from the older couple at the next table and they stand to leave. The old man slaps his paper down on the table, open to the story he was reading. The door chimes as they exit and I stand to follow. I glance down at the paper.

EMILY SUTTON RETURNS AFTER FIVE YEARS

I finish the rest of my water and shrug. "At least it wasn't on the front page." I scoop my cell phone and keys from the table and say goodbye.

I make my way down the brick steps outside the cafe to my car, and queue up my running playlist on my phone, desperate to

THE TURN

release the ache building inside my chest. I'm distracted, and as I turn the corner towards the parking lot, I must have misjudged my steps because I slam straight into a wall.

15

EMILY

"Emily! Are you alright?" I can't believe my luck. It's Sawyer, hovering over me, helping me up from the sidewalk, and I'm sure I look an absolute mess.

"I'm fine. Sorry, I didn't see you there." I fidget with my nails self-consciously.

"It's no problem. Where are you off to in such a hurry?" Sawyer is tipping his face pointedly, trying to force my eye contact.

I glance back in the direction of the cafe and mutter something unintelligible about meeting some old friends. I'll look anywhere to avoid staring at the way the soft waves in his hair lay perfectly off to the side, framing his eyes beautifully beneath them, which he's somehow managed to accomplish without gobs of product. His brow furrows and I try again. "I was just about to go for a run. I was getting my playlist ready on my phone. I didn't see you."

Sawyer grins and pinches his lips together. God, it's adorable when he does that. He interrupts my idiotic drooling when I notice he looks as though he's about to burst into hysterics any second.

"What?" I ask. He just shakes his head gently so I ask again. "What's so funny?"

Sawyer straightens and clears his throat, stifling his amusement. He flashes a brilliantly white smile and it's the closest I've ever felt to understanding what it means when a woman swoons. "Nothing. Sorry, it's just . . . I'm trying to picture you running." He's failed at hiding his amusement and his laugh is full and warm, heating me from the inside out. "I don't think I could have paid the Emily Wilks I knew to run."

I roll my eyes playfully. "I'm a fantastic runner, thank you very much."

He nods enthusiastically as he gathers his composure, just a hint of a smirk still tugging at the corner of his mouth. "Oh, I'm sure you are a phenomenal runner."

"Anyway, I hate it." I stuff my phone into my back pocket. "But I find that it's helpful when I'm feeling tense, so I do it."

"Then you can't hate it that much."

Do I hate it? I consider his point. "Well, I don't do it right. I listen to the wrong music."

Sawyer doesn't reply. Instead, he holds out his palm.

"What's that? What do you want?"

"Hand it over," he orders.

"Hand what over?"

"Your playlist. You said you were looking at it on your phone. Let's see what you're working with." He waits, never dropping his hand.

I reach back into my pocket and drag the phone out slowly. "Alright, but wait. You can't judge what's on there." I slap the phone into his palm and watch as he scrolls down the list of songs.

His sly grin appears once more and he looks out from under his lashes. "Justin Bieber? The Biebs? A bit teenybopper, isn't he?" I swat his shoulder.

"I'm sure Raina could attest that he has some really great songs. And anyway, you said you wouldn't judge!"

"Actually, you *told* me not to judge. I agreed to no such thing. Can't believe you're a Belieber . . ."

I roll my eyes again, more viciously and it occurs to me where Harley learned this particular skill. "Seems to me that you might be a closeted fan yourself, since you even know the term 'belieber'. Whatever, it works. The normal workout beats don't do it for me. I have to feel something real when I work out if I want to get the most out of it."

Sawyer passes my phone back to me. "I like to run too."

I can't resist the urge to try to dish him some sass right back. "Yeah? And what kind of stellar jams do you listen to? Let me guess. Eminem? Nelly?"

If I'm not mistaken, Sawyers cheeks glow with the slightest pink tint as he drops his eyes to the ground. He looks up, ignoring my question. "Will you send me your playlist?" I'm caught off guard, unsure why he wants it. He must think I'm waiting to hear the magic word because he adds a quick "Please."

I nod. "Fine, but you have to send me one of yours too." If he's going to rip apart my music, then I'm going to be ready to do the same.

"Deal. I won't erase anything, just adds. I promise." Sawyer extends a hand and we shake on it. "Well, I'll let you get to your workout. But it was good running into you."

I walk around him and then turn to face him with a shy smile. Can he tell that he makes my stomach flutter? There's no way he can't hear my pulse hammering in my throat when he's near. He's anything but stupid, though that's exactly how I feel for indulging this little crush that every woman must have on him. I'm one of hundreds. Regardless, I admit there's a certain excitement in feeling this way again, so what's the harm? It's not as if my heart can break any more than it already has. "Yeah, it was." I take a step backwards and Sawyer glances down at my feet, likely just making sure I do, indeed, know how to walk, or run for that matter. "Have fun . . . doing whatever it was you were off to do. Sorry that I kept you."

He brushes off my apology. "I was just grabbing coffee. Nothing critical."

"Ah, that's where you're wrong. Coffee absolutely is a critical matter." That earns a chuckle from Sawyer. I soak it in as he begins to walk backward.

"See you later, Em." Sawyer's smile reaches the corners of his eyes.

I take one more tentative step back. "Later?"

"We have a private lesson today, right?"

I spark of realization hits me. Harley. "Right! Yes, of course. See you then." My face flushes and I spin around to hightail it to my car, feeling Sawyer's eyes burning into me while I mutter curses at myself under my breath.

"Bye, Em!" I hear him call out and I throw a wave over my shoulder without looking back.

16

EMILY

I see the road coming up as my feet hammer against the pavement. I won't avoid it this time. I ran this route on purpose. Something about my visit with Zola and Annalee is nagging at me. Tugging at some invisible string in my mind, a connection I can't quite make. Then, maybe it isn't something about our chat. Perhaps it's the whole damn thing.

Moore Road. I can see the sign.

I hadn't expected to become so touchy, but the eyes around us rattled me. I know our children went through enough during the trial, more than any child should have to endure. But something about Annalee's particular brand of defensiveness, the way she still wrote me off so quickly, after all this time, is bothering me. I wasn't asking to question the boys; I'd never drag them though it all again. Not when they're doing so well. Not unless I was absolutely certain. And that's the problem with avoidance. I'm not sure how certain I am anymore. But I do know I won't avoid it anymore.

Only another thirty paces or so.

In my efforts to shield Harley, and myself, the assurance I was once filled with became murky. In that, I stopped fighting for him, my son. I stopped pushing for the truth and instead turned my sights on self-preservation. The guilt of moving on is rooted too deeply within me now. I know that I'll never be entirely free of it, but even still, being here brings it all racing to the surface.

I slow to a walk as the street signs at the crossroads float over my head. I can see the bend in the road.

I came back for you, Ryan. I'm here.

Moore Road looks bright with the late morning sun shining behind me. The exact opposite of that day. Everything else looks exactly the way it did before. The grass is dry and yellow, the trees are lush, but the branches look brittle in the summer heat. There are only two lanes on this section of the road, with hardly any shoulder. I walk along the side of the road taking it all in.

In a flash, I'm back behind the wheel again, looking out through the windshield. I know what comes next. Therapy has taught me that this particular fantasy of mine is a coping mechanism.

Up ahead, I see them. A group of boys riding their bicycles toward me. The sun is beginning to dip down behind them creating a backlight that obscures their faces, even as I approach, but I'm wearing sunglasses to combat the glare. A couple of them are too far out, damn near straddling the paint dividing the two lanes. Why are they out so far? Don't they see the car approaching? I begin to slow my vehicle as a bend in the road comes nearer, and I see the group move to the side of the road and into safety. I relax as I make the turn.

In my memories, I always rewrite the ending, begging the universe to give me a different outcome. Because that isn't what happened at all, and I didn't come here today to pretend otherwise. I came here to remember.

Reality and court transcripts will tell you that at 6:35 p.m. one evening in April 2015, I was driving home from visiting Zola. When I turned onto Moore Road, the sun was blinding but I deemed it safer to squint and keep my eyes on the road than to root around for a pair of sunglasses. As I approached the bend in the road, the sun shifted just enough that I could see. I wasn't speeding, but the speed limit also didn't require me to slow down when making that turn. When I exited the turn, I flicked my eyes upwards, looking out ahead of me rather than down at the outer edge of the road. And then I saw them. A group of boys, faces hidden in shadows from the sun setting behind them, riding too far out in the road. I screamed from inside my car, begging them to move out of the road, and that's when I saw the foot shoot out. The one that kicked another boy directly into my path. There was no time to process anything other than slamming on the brake and praying they moved in time. Only after I stopped, did I understand what happened.

I keep walking down the road, the bend creeping closer. When I'm nearly there, where it happened, I look down. The road is marred by several pairs of skid marks. This turn has been a problem for many others. Logically, I know that these marks weren't made by my tires. Too much time has passed for that to be true. But they still feel too familiar.

Tears fill my eyes as I try to focus, but my legs are weak and unsteady. I collapse into a crouch and the tears fall, blotting the pavement beneath me. I look up, trying to see them again. Trying to remember. I was sure I saw four of them staring back at me. *Yes, there's Charlie and Beck. I'm yelling at them to get my phone and call 9-1-1. Tristan finally moves to my car. But where did the other boy go? There should be five bicycles on the ground around us. One bicycle is pinned beneath my car, but I only see three, laying on the ground near the shoulder, one nearly on top of another,*

THE TURN

the third behind them as if this were the order in which they were riding.

Could the boy have ridden away quickly enough that I didn't notice? Why didn't the other boys, our boys, back me up in the courthouse? I'm trying so hard to see what I'm missing, but there's nothing there. All I see is grief, and loss. I allow myself a few minutes to fall apart before I pick myself back up and run home, where my daughter is waiting for me.

17

HARLEY

Raina won't stop talking, even though Coach Sawyer had told us about a million times that if we don't get to work, we'll spend the hour running laps. He has yet to follow through. I think it's because he's too busy talking to my mom.

"So what was your last school like? Lincoln is so small. I've been with the same kids practically my whole life."

I kind of love how dramatic Raina is. "Didn't you just move here from Sacramento, like a few years ago?" I ask.

"Yeah, but you know what I mean. It must have been so different in Folsom. It's such a big place."

I shrug. "It wasn't that much bigger. Anyway, it's not that great having such a big school. I didn't really know anybody that well. I had friends on the soccer team but outside of that, not many."

"So then, are you glad you moved back here?" Raina asks. It takes me a minute to consider whether I'm glad. No one has ever asked me what I thought. When we moved to Folsom, mom just told me that's what was happening. And it was the same moving back here.

"I think I am. My best friend growing up lived here and I missed her a lot when we left. All of my best memories are from here. But . . . I don't know. I'm also like, kind of nervous. I was really close to a group of people here before but now it's been years since we've talked. I just haven't even thought about what it would be like if I ever saw them again. It's like I'm starting all over but there is also all this baggage. Does that make any sense?" I reach for my toes to stretch out my hamstrings. I can't even begin to sort out my feelings about possibly seeing the boys again. What if I have to revisit all these secrets I haven't had to think about all this time? Will they come out? It feels disloyal to Ryan's memory even considering it.

"So your best friend still lives here then?" Raina follows my movements.

I shake my head. "Not sure. We didn't keep in touch after that."

"That's weird," Raina muses. "So, why did you guys leave anyway if you loved it here so much?"

"Girls!" A sharp whistle from Coach Sawyer tells us we've spent long enough stretching and it's time to start shooting drills.

I climb to my feet and reach a hand down to help Raina up. "My brother died." I start jogging over to where a stash of soccer balls waits for us and line up my first shot. I back up a few steps and prepare to strike but I'm wrapped up in a hug before I can move.

"God, Harley. I'm so sorry." Raina lets me go. "Were you close?"

I dip my chin down. "Yeah, he was the best brother a girl could ask for."

"If you ever want to talk about it, I'm here."

"Thanks. It was a long time ago. But, I'll let you know if I do." I stride forward and strike the ball hard. It flies over the crossbar.

Damn. I picked my head up at the last second, leaning too far back to check my alignment. Rookie mistake.

Coach Sawyer shouts from where he's standing. "Keep your head down, eyes on the ball, not on the goal. The goal isn't going anywhere." I throw a quick look of acknowledgment that I heard him, stuffing down the urge to yell I already knew that, and run off to retrieve my ball while Raina takes a turn.

When she lines back up behind me, she leans forward and whispers in my ear, "Look at them. They're kind of adorable together, right?"

I track her line of sight to find my mom standing way too close to Coach Sawyer with a goofy grin plastered on her face. She does look happy. I nod. "My mom has a crush on your dad."

"Ohmygawd! You think? Because my dad totally has it bad for her. He was telling me all about how they knew each other as kids and how it was so fun to run into an old friend. It was so sus." Raina laughs way too loud, earning a glare from Coach Sawyer.

We line up our next shots from a cone on the other side of the penalty box. We both make those shots and between the time it takes Raina to get her ball and line up behind me again, she's come up with the brilliant plan to get our parents together. "We could be sisters!" She squeals, grabbing my forearm.

I have to admit, I don't hate the idea. I've spent so long missing people I love. First Ryan, then Theo. I like Raina a lot, and she's here. It'd be nice if she stayed here.

"We can try." I concede and Raina is thrilled.

We make it through the rest of practice and avoid Coach Sawyer's pretend wrath, but before we leave, Raina and I agree to begin encouraging the idea of dating. Or at least spending a little time together off the turf.

18

EMILY

Harley and I are eating lunch in the kitchen, talking about what to expect when she starts school next month when a knock on the door startles me. We haven't had any visitors since we moved back and after the unwelcome sign painted on our door, I'm curious, but also a bit anxious to see who it is.

I tell Harley to stay in the kitchen and I make my way to the door not sure who to expect. When I look through the peephole, my shoulders sag, and I swing the door open.

"Bryce. What are you doing here?"

Bryce waits a moment before asking whether he can come inside.

I don't have a great reason for keeping him on the porch, so I step to the side and close the door behind him.

Harley comes out of the kitchen and trots up to him. Bryce wraps her up in a hug. "Hey Hart." He pushes her back to arm's length and crinkles his nose. "I'm guessing you just got back from soccer practice."

Harley chuckles and rolls her eyes.

"So?" I ask. "What are you doing here?"

Bryce pretends to look wounded. "Can't I come by to see my two best girls when I'm in town?"

Harley smiles. "Of course—"

"No. Actually, you can't just swing by whenever you feel like it," I say at the same time.

"Why not?" Bryce asks, throwing his arms open.

"Because . . . it's rude. You don't live here. And you threw away the privilege of seeing us whenever you like when you threw away our family." I scramble for more excuses since a father dropping by to see his daughter isn't exactly a bad thing. Just because I'm mad at him, doesn't mean Harley has to be too. The thought jars the realization that Harley is standing next to me. I pull back a bit and reset. "What if we had company?"

Bryce looks at me, a skeptical grin on his face. "And what company might that be?"

Harley waits and I watch her eyes flicker back and forth between her father and me. "Coach Sawyer and Raina?" She offers innocently.

My jaw falls open as Bryce jumps on this information. "Your coach comes over to your house?" He drags his eyes slowly up to meet mine, accusations and assumptions swimming in his honey-colored irises.

Harley looks as though she's about to add onto this tenuous situation she's created. I stop her before she can start. "No, he does not come to the house. He never has. Sawyer is a professional."

"Uh huh . . ." Bryce sucks on his teeth. "Well, I just came by to see if I could help you find that box you were looking for."

Before I can stop him, Bryce marches into Ryan's room. I follow him and watch as he steps into Ryan's closet. "I don't know why Harley said that." The guilt that bubbles up is unintentional. As angry as I am, I still care about him. I don't think he'd be able to rattle me this way if I didn't. Bryce is Harley's father and there was so much love between us for so long. Seeing him hurt is complicated, to say the least. I hate everything about the way he handled things between us after Ryan died. Why couldn't he just be there when I actually needed him? I don't need him anymore, and now all he seems to want to do is stay.

"It doesn't matter. It's none of my business what you do with your free time." He pulls a cardboard box down from a shelf. "It hasn't been for a long time, right?" He pops open the top and digs for a moment before drawing out a navy-blue storage box and setting it on the bed. "Is this the box you wanted?"

I nod. "Yup. Looks like you knew right where to find it." I say it pointedly, remembering how much he insisted on the phone that he hadn't a clue as to its location.

He lets out a deep sigh. "I just remembered that I packed some things up, and I thought it might be here."

"A phone call would have sufficed in that case," I press.

He stands upright and walks toward the doorframe where I'm still standing with my arms folded. "Next time I'll call first." I step to the side so he can get by and he makes his way down the hallway. He's halfway to the front door when he stops and turns back towards me. "I know you're still angry with me. But I didn't do any of this to hurt you." He waves a hand in the air, gesturing generically to the house, or possibly to his affair that still hangs heavy in the air between us. "I hope you realize that one day."

I watch as he goes back to the kitchen and talks to Harley

before they exchange goodbyes, and I ask Harley to lock the door behind him.

Back in Ryan's room, I make my way over to the dark-blue box, and gently lift the lid. Bryce is trying to put the pieces of our life back together, trying to make up for what he did. And for what he didn't do. I know him so well. He's hoping that if he pretends like everything is fine for long enough, maybe I'll decide it's fine, too. What he can't understand is that I don't want it back. It was hard enough losing Ryan. Not having Bryce in my corner when I really needed him, and then to have him step out with that woman . . . he said she didn't mean anything to him, that he was hurting and lost. But she was worth destroying what was left of us. Seeing Bryce is a constant reminder of what it was like before. When Ryan was here.

Bryce ruined everything and I can't stand it.

I look down expecting to see Ryan's mementos, memories of his summers with his best friends, but the box is empty. I sigh and put it back in the cardboard box Bryce pulled down.

When I close the box top, a smear of red flashes before my eye. Did Bryce cut himself when he opened the box? I didn't notice him flinch, not when he opened the box, not when he stuffed his hands into his pockets. I lean in. Upon closer inspection, I realize that it's not blood. It's paint.

19

EMILY
Friday, August 6, 2021

On the way to Harley's soccer lesson, I'm still thinking about Bryce's visit over a week ago. I can't find a single reason why he'd paint the word "murderer" on our front door. I realize I haven't been the kindest to him, but I still don't think he would do that to me. He certainly wouldn't do that to Harley. While he didn't stand up for me the way I needed him to, he certainly never seemed to openly blame me for what happened. Or maybe I just wasn't paying close enough attention. Anyway, I found no other traces of red paint in or around the house. I planned to confront him about it, but when I asked if he'd happened to have left any red paint around the house that I could use, he seemed genuinely confused, so I dropped it, telling myself I'd come back to it when I had some solid proof that the paint on our door was Bryce's doing. I don't even know if Bryce is aware that someone tagged our door, unless maybe Harley mentioned it to him. Red paint could have gotten on that box lid long before Bryce packed up Ryan's things. Though I also can't figure out why he bothered to pack up an empty storage box, like a box shaped Russian doll.

    I force myself to put this aside and focus on Harley's lesson. She's been working with Sawyer twice a week for almost six weeks now. He's been a great match as a coach for Harley. He keeps the sport fun, and he really sees her and has learned how to push her with kindness to pull the best out of her. I've grown quite fond of these sessions, and of Raina, who's been a great friend to Harley. They've become quite close. It's been a joy to watch them bond while they work on mastering their individual skills. I've tried to get Zola to bring Theo around for a reunion with Harley, but between the girls extracurriculars and our work schedules, we simply haven't been able to make anything work yet. Harley must be missing her best friend. She never seemed to let anyone else get close to her after we moved away. However, Raina seems to have filled that void for Harley. And Raina seems to feel the same kinship towards Harley.

    When we walk into the arena, there's an odd tension in the air. Raina is sitting quietly, stretching off to the side while Sawyer is on the phone with someone, and the conversation doesn't sound like it's going well.

    Though I can't hear everything he's saying, his posture is rigid and his right arm alternates between flailing wildly and rubbing the back of his neck. "Damn it! Please don't do this!" Sawyer snaps. I'm not sure who he's talking to or what they're doing, but Sawyer isn't happy about it. I watch as his head falls back, and he gives in. "Yeah. Yeah, alright. I'll be here. Alright, bye." He stuffs his phone into his pocket and laces his fingers behind his head. I look at Harley who is having a silent conversation with Raina across the way. I watch as Raina mouths something to Harley and Harley makes eyes back at her. I wait until I snag Harley's attention and I motion to her with my chin, quietly telling her to go over and get started.

When Harley jogs by Sawyer, he looks startled. He whirls around to face me. "Em! Sorry, I didn't know you were here."

"No problem. Is everything okay?" I ask.

His face droops. "Yeah, sorry about that. You clearly overheard. It's nothing. I'm glad you guys are here." He turns towards Harley. "Be ready to go in five minutes, sound good?" Harley nods at him and resumes talking quietly to Raina as they stretch.

The lesson is half over, and while Sawyer was able to reset after his phone call, he's been slowly unraveling, unusually frustrated with the girls when they mess up a drill or snicker to each other. When Harley shanks a fifth shot with her weak foot, Sawyer's remaining composure dissolves. "Harley! How many times do I have to tell you to strike with the laces, head down? Why is that so difficult for you today?" I watch as Harley's face drops and she turns her back to him and walks over to where her bag is sitting. I recognize the way her shoulders shake when she's trying not to cry, and I call out to Sawyer. He drags a hand down his face as he makes his way over to me.

He looks defeated. I would never normally insert myself into their practice, but Sawyer is visibly out of sorts and I'm concerned, both about him and the mark it will leave on today's session. "Look, I'm not sure what's going on with you today, but you can't lay into Harley like that. I'm not opposed to some tough love, but this? Berating her doesn't work. You know that. She's going to crumble." I don't want to come down on him too hard. He looks like he's doing that pretty well all on his own. But I do need him to know where the boundary lies when it comes to my kid.

Sawyer nods. "I know."

"She likes you. She'll work for you just because you ask her to. You don't have to be a drill sergeant with her. And to be honest, it doesn't seem like you." I duck my head into his line of vision and force his eyes to meet mine so that he can see that I'm not angry. "Do you want to tell me what's going on?"

"I'm sorry. It's just . . ." He looks as if he's deciding something. Maybe whether he can trust me, or how much he wants to share. "It's my sister. Her kid has been giving her a hard time for the last few years and his dad isn't any help. She wants me to take Jeremey in for a while. I know she's at her wit's end but I just don't think passing him off is the best decision." He glances off to the side.

I tilt my head to meet his eyes once more and show him that I'm paying attention. "Anyway, she's going to drop Jeremey off here. She was going to pass him off no matter what I said so I told her I'd take him. I figured it was better than whoever else she might find. Maybe I can help him. I don't know." He pauses and looks over at Raina who appears to be giving Harley a pep talk. "I messed up. I'll go talk to Harley."

Before he leaves, I reach out and put a hand on his arm. "Thank you for sharing. For what it's worth, I think your nephew is lucky to have you in his corner."

"Thanks, Em." Sawyer looks down at where my hand rests on his tattooed skin and smiles. Then he leaves to talk to Harley and Raina.

The slate is wiped clean, and the rest of the lesson goes smoothly. Harley gets her head back in the game and Sawyer relaxes his approach. As the girls wrap up and head back to their bags to change out of their cleats, the doors to the arena fly open and a woman comes marching in, a teenage boy trailing behind her defiantly. I recognize his sister, Landry, though I haven't seen her in nearly thirty years. She looks furious. I call Harley over to me, but she waves me off and stays on the opposite side of the turf chatting with Raina. I train my eyes on my daughter to give Sawyer and Landry the illusion of privacy.

They talk seriously for only a minute or two before Landry storms out, not bothering to say goodbye to the boy who is left standing alone, clutching a duffle bag.

I watch as Harley makes her way slowly over to me, her eyes never leaving Sawyer and his nephew. A quick glance reveals Sawyer leaning in to hug his nephew. Sawyer's back is to me and when his nephew returns the hug, I get my first look at Jeremey's face. He's tall and lean. I would guess he is perhaps still a teen, since his mother is passing him off rather than simply kicking him out of her house. His hair is dark, wavy, and just long enough that the front locks drape over one eye. There is something strangely familiar about him.

I glance over to make sure Harley is still making her way to me. She is still focused on the pair of them, though I can't quite decipher the look on her face which seems equal parts interested and anxious. She's had a stressful practice though and I chalk it up to that.

But when I look back over at Sawyer, Jeremey's eyes are pinning me in place, a curious smirk painted across his face. A chill racks my bones as the realization settles in, exactly why he looks so familiar. My eyes squeeze shut and I go back to the accident. I look around, searching for the missing boy. The one who kicked my son into the road. I see the shape of his blurry face, and a mop of short, dark curls sitting on top of his head. My heart pounds inside my chest and my eyes flutter open once more, finding Jeremey, who continues to stare at me over Sawyer's shoulder.

20

EMILY

Harley barely says a word on the way home. It isn't like her. Most days she can't stop talking about what she did wrong or how she can step up her game next lesson. Typically, she'd detail out the drills she plans to incorporate over the next few days and start listing different players who are strong in those particular areas. Her silence is unsettling.

"Hey, you. Are you doing alright?"

Harley seems to snap back from wherever her mind was. "Huh?"

"You're awfully quiet. I was asking if you were okay."

"Yeah, I'm fine. Just thinking."

I glance at her, trying to read her mood, but her poker face is improving. "Anything you want to talk about?" Harley shakes her head and turns back to face her window.

My fingers begin to drum on the steering wheel. Once Harley's mind is set, it's nearly impossible to draw her back out from her retreat until she's ready. But, I'm her mother, so I try again. "So, what was the look on your face when Coach Sawyer's nephew showed up?"

Harley's head whips around in a flash and if I wasn't curious about her reaction to Jeremey's arrival before, I am now. Her brows knit together. "What do you mean?"

"You couldn't seem to take your eyes off of Sawyer and Jeremey when you were walking towards me. What was going through your mind?"

Harley huffs out a sigh. "Oh, nothing really. Coach apologized for being an assho—"

"Harley Rae Sutton!"

Harley raises her arms in surrender. "Coach said it! Not me." I pinch my lips closed in exasperation. Great. Just great.

"Anyway . . . Coach apologized for being a jerk and explained he was frustrated about whatever the situation is with his nephew. I was just curious, that's all."

I don't quite buy her explanation, but I let her retreat back into herself for the moment. I can't blame her for being curious. I was, too. I can't stop seeing the look on Jeremey's face. Can't shake the feeling that he sees me too, somehow.

"Why don't you ever date?" Harley asks without peeling her eyes from the scenery whipping past the glass beside her. It takes a moment to register her words, draining all other thoughts from my head so I can process this question she's never asked before.

"Where did that come from?" I volley back to her to buy myself some time.

"You and Dad have been divorced for years. Dad dates. So why don't you?"

"Your dad is dating?" I assumed that after his affair, and the way he's been clinging to me that maybe he'd realized he has no business getting involved in a romantic relationship. He's dating. I can't decide how I feel about that, whether I care or if it's just strange to know after so long. Regardless, it's supremely irritating that I'll now have to have a chat with Bryce about the whole thing. Forget the way he perched there up on his high horse when he thought that I might be seeing Sawyer romantically. The fact that he finds no issue with bringing random women I've never met around our daughter, without so much as mentioning it in passing to me during his pit stops to the house, is worrisome. And what if she gets attached to one of them? What happens when that woman abandons her too? What if that woman is cruel to her?

What if one of them tries to take Harley away from me?

Harley is immune to my stalling. "Don't change the subject. But yeah, he dates." Her attitude is pure nonchalance.

I consider why I never started dating again. I told myself I was busy working and raising my daughter. But maybe that's not quite true. "I really don't know, Harley. It's not something I think much about." I pause, considering why I don't ever think about it. "I'm just so busy, and I like spending my time with you. Besides, I haven't dated in forever." I snort. "Even if I wanted to, I don't think I'd know how anymore."

She turns to face me so I know she means what she says next. "Well, you could though, you know? If you did want to, it'd be alright with me."

"Are you so eager to get rid of me?" I joke. Insert eye roll in three, two . . .

"Mom . . ."

I still know her. "Just kidding. Thanks, kiddo. I'll keep that in mind."

Harley nods. "What about Coach Sawyer?"

Oh no. "What about Coach Sawyer?" I have to tread carefully here because any fool can see where this is headed.

"Do you like him? Because Raina said he totally likes you and he told her all about how you two were practically best friends growing up."

I chuff. "That is a gross exaggeration. We lived on the same street for a long time, but he was a couple years older than me, and we hardly spoke."

"That's not what Raina said."

I laugh outright at that. "Raina is fourteen years old and teenage girls tend to be a little dramatic, in case you didn't know." I wink at her.

"But—"

"But nothing." I shake my head. "There's really nothing to tell, so how about we table this discussion for the foreseeable future. Cool?"

Harley throws her head back against her seat and relents. "Ugh, fine." Harley smacks her hands on her legs, drumming out a beat. When her hands still, she speaks again. "Why didn't you want to tell Coach Sawyer about Ryan?"

"What?"

"At our first lesson, when I tried to explain why we moved back, you cut me off. And then last week, Raina was totally shocked when I told her I had a brother who died. If she didn't know, I'm assuming Coach Sawyer doesn't either."

"Aw, Harley," I start, woefully unprepared for this turn in conversation. "I don't know. I guess I just wasn't ready. I don't want that to be the first thing every new person learns about us. It colors a person's perception of you. It changes how they act around you, and how they talk to you. I guess . . . I guess I just wanted to be treated normally, and not like I'm fragile. Does that make sense?" Harley nods. "And I don't care that you told Raina, either. It's your life to share, too, whenever you want."

Harley doesn't answer me, and I change the subject because I never like to close a discussion with tension. "Are you excited for dinner tonight?" We agreed to meet at Annalee's house for dinner. "I know that Theo is excited to see you."

"Do you think she even remembers me?" Harley asks seriously.

I know Harley was heartbroken to leave Theo behind. It's my fault that they didn't keep in touch after we moved. I wonder, again, if I made the right decision for us or if I turned what was already a heartbreaking mess into something even more tragic. But maybe it's not too late to fix things. "Of course she remembers you! How could she forget you?"

Harley smiles, looking genuinely happy at the thought. "I'm excited. A little nervous to see everyone again, but I think dinner will be great."

I turn into our neighborhood, pushing thoughts of Jeremey and of dating out of my mind as I pull the car into the driveway. "I think so too."

21

EMILY

Harley and I are the last to arrive at Annalee's house that evening. While we all live within three minutes of each other, I suspect that Zola was told to arrive earlier so that they could give the kids a briefing, preparing for our arrival. I should stop calling them "the kids". The boys are going on eighteen years old, and Theo is a teenager herself. The idea is solidified in my mind when the front door flies open and we are faced with a mountain of a young man, built like a brick wall, and just as familiar as the day we met.

I can feel the shock smear across my face. "Tristan! My god, look at you! How did this happen?" Before I can get another word in, he wraps me in a warm hug briefly then steps back, a genuine smile beaming at us that reaches from ear to ear. It's comforting to see that despite everything, Tristan is still the same affectionate, happy boy he's always been. A stranger to no one, best friend to all. "It's so good to see you."

I step inside the house, revealing Harley who's been hidden

behind me. I turn to see her raise a tentative hand at Tristan that he quickly disregards. He scoops her up in his arms and spins her around on the porch. As she whips by me, her eyes are wide with surprise and I can't help but laugh at the two of them as she quickly melts into giggles, like no time has passed. "My god, Hart! I can't believe it. You're all grown up!" I hear her mumble a response as Tristan lifts her arms out wide and twirls her around. When the boys found out that her dad called her Hart, they adopted the nickname too, much to Harley's chagrin. She always said it made her feel like a little kid, but I think that's why they liked it. She was a little sister to each of them. The familiar use of her nickname is a sweet sound coming from Tristan.

"Tristan, is that them?" Annalee calls out from another room. We make our way down the hall together and into the living room where everyone else is waiting to swarm us.

Theo is on her feet in an instant and barreling straight for Harley. Both girls squeal in delight and begin jumping up and down in a way I've not seen Harley do in years. I turn toward the figure making their way over to me before I begin to cry. "Beck! Is that you?" My jaw falls open at the sight of him. He grins at me, his dark hair swept neatly to one side, Nordic-blue eyes sparkling. He's thin but as I hug him tight, I can feel that he's filled out with lean muscle as if he runs track. I just can't believe this is the boy that used to walk around the cottage in a lab coat and goggles trying to explain anatomy to us. I step back and grab Beck under the chin and smile at him. "Congratulations on your acceptance into UC Davis. I'm so happy for you. I want to hear all about your plans for senior year tonight, yeah?"

Beck nods coolly even as his cheeks bloom pink. "Of course." He reaches in for one more hug before moving to the side, and I see him. Charlie.

Charlie is standing next to the couch with his hands tucked away behind his back. His hair has grown out into soft waves and his eyes dart to the floor as if he can't quite look at me. I make me way over to him and wrap him in my arms, soaking him in. A living, breathing reminder of my son. All of the boys were close, but the bond between Ryan and Charlie was special. They looked out for each other, stayed up late talking about everything young boys talked about, and they took care of their little sisters in a way that Beck and Tristan didn't understand how to do. Theo and Harley grew to become like little sisters to them all, but they belonged to Charlie and Ryan, and the boys took that responsibility seriously.

I hold Charlie for a long time, until I feel the eyes on us. Charlie must feel it too, but he doesn't try to move until I release him. His eyes finally meet mine and my tears fill to the point of overflow. I swipe the tears away and I grab his hand and fold it between my own. "Thank you for coming tonight, Charlie. I can't tell you what it means to me."

Charlie's eyes fall to the floor again for a minute and when I let go of his hand, it flies into his pocket. "How could I not?" He smiles but it's stiff and sad.

We all go about exchanging pleasantries and eventually make our way into the dining area where Zola and I help Annalee set the table, family style while the kids—children? Young people? Screw it—while the kids continue to chat animatedly around the table. All of them except for Charlie who sits there, replying politely when spoken to but contributing nothing more. I watch as he provides appropriately timed, but empty, smiles. He looks wary of it all as if he's afraid to be too happy. If only I could tell him just how deeply I understand. I could sit with him and explain how it feels like I walk along a flimsy thread threatening to snap at any moment. And I would unravel along with it. But maybe we can weather this if we hold onto each other. I think Ryan would have wanted that. He would want us to be happy. Or at least to try. Looking around the table, I *want* to try again. With all of them.

The table grows louder by the minute as everyone competes to be heard. Annalee sits at the head of the table, Tristan at the other end. I sit next to Annalee with Harley on my right, Theo on her other side. Directly across from me is Charlie, and next to him sits Beck, and then finally Zola. We take turns catching each other up on what we've been up to, treading the delicate line between enthusiasm and intending not to appear too happy given who's very noticeable missing tonight.

No one mentions Ryan.

Whether from fear of ruining a pleasant evening, or of making someone cry, or of having to rehash the trauma that ripped us apart, not a single one of us mentions him. Regardless of our reasons, his name isn't spoken, as if he doesn't exist. In spite of all that, Ryan's presence looms largely over the entire night. Or is it his absence?

Dessert is brought out. A coconut cream pie. Annalee remembered that it's—was—Ryan's favorite. We pass around slices of the pie, oohing and aahing over how delicious it is.

No one mentions Ryan.

Zola heads into the kitchen where she helps Annalee do the dishes. I overhear them talking together, swapping recipes and tips to getting just the right cook on a tri-tip. The kids are swapping sports stories at the table.

No one mentions Ryan.

When I move to help clear the table, Zola and Annalee insist that I relax, and I tell them I'll argue with them about it after I use the restroom. I step inside and lock the door behind me before leaning on the counter and taking a few deep breaths.

No one mentioned Ryan.

I want to scream because it isn't fair that Ryan isn't here, and everyone should be ashamed of themselves for pretending like everything is fine now. For acting like it hasn't made any difference. I know my anger is misplaced. It isn't like I made a point of talking about him either. It's why I came in here to collect myself. They're nervous, unsure of how to act around me.

I want them to be happy. They should be happy. Ryan would have wanted that. We just have to figure out how to be together again, without him.

I hear Theo and Harley walk past the bathroom door. Harley is telling Theo about Raina and how much she thinks Theo would love her. Raina is great, though not as great as Theo. Harley is careful to add that. Their voices fade as they pass by, and they must have gone outside because I hear the back door slam. I right myself and I turn on the sink to splash cool water on my face and wash my hands. When I shut the faucet off, the girls' voices float into the room once more, and I notice that the bathroom window is open. I smile at the sound of them together again, but my smile slips when I hear Jeremey's name.

"Are you sure it was him? Like, absolutely sure?" Theo asks.

Harley grunts out a noise. "One hundred percent."

I hear a tiny gasp escape from Theo. "Oh my god. Does your mom know?"

Do I know what? Do I know Jeremey? Does my daughter? Did Raina tell Harley something? Whatever it is that Harley knows about Jeremey, I am certain I do not. I lean forward on the counter to listen better, but my hands slip on the surface because I forgot to dry them. My arm bangs on the countertop, knocking over a soap dispenser and a bottle of hand lotion. Their voices go silent. Damn it. I scramble to clean up the mess I made and exit the bathroom before they come back inside. I need to find out what Harley told Theo about Jeremey. I think back to seeing him at Harley's soccer practice, and how his smirk immediately put me on edge. All along I assumed the other boy was just a random tagalong kid that the boys picked up somewhere. But maybe I've been wrong. Maybe he's more, a friend even. How close was he to the group? How could I not have known him? None of the other mothers knew him either. Did they? I've questioned whether he was simply a bystander, a witness to a horrific tragedy. Now this. This all but confirms it for me. He's the child that pushed my son into the road. If Harley knows him, if she knows this about him . . . is my daughter in danger too?

By the time I get back to the dining room, the table has been cleared and Zola and Annalee appear to have everything under control in the kitchen as they chat. Annalee washes and passes the dishes to Zola, who either hand dries them or loads them into the dishwasher. The sight makes me ache. It's not jealousy, not exactly, but something reminiscent of it. My absence pushed them closer and they seem like they've found a new rhythm all together. Another thing that I missed out on and now that I'm here, I wonder if there's space for me anymore.

I look to my left and I see Charlie sitting on the couch in the living room again, alone. I walk over and plop down next to him with a huge sigh and it feels like release. I lay my head back and close my eyes. When I open them, I look straight ahead, and Charlie speaks. "This kind of sucks."

I know exactly what he means, and I tell him as much. "It totally sucks."

He turns his head towards me, but he doesn't meet my eyes, rather appearing to look just past me to the other side of the couch. "I don't feel right without Ryan here," Charlie says quietly.

"Me neither." Charlie's head falls to my shoulder. He feels so young again, so small, and I let him rest there as long as he wants, grateful for his courage to miss Ryan out loud. Charlie has always been an extension of Ryan and I hadn't realized just how much I missed this boy until now. He feels like getting a tiny piece of my heart back.

Voices sound behind us and Charlie's head snaps back up as the rest of our makeshift family files into the room with us. It's getting late and I really should be getting Harley home after a hard day. We could both use a little extra rest. I'm about to say so but Annalee is distracted by the fact that Tristan has spilled some pasta sauce on his shirt and surely the stain has set by now.

"Go change your shirt so I can get some Shout on this one," she instructs him and Tristan hustles back to his room only to reemerge in an old hoodie he's cut the sleeves from, that Annalee also disapproves of. "Honestly, Tristan, do you own any clothing that isn't covered in grass stains or paint?"

Tristan shrugs her off. "Mom, you're the only one who's bothered by it. Anyway, looks like Hart and Emily are getting ready to leave." He tosses his head in our direction as we're huddled together near the entryway.

"It's true, we need to get going but this has been lovely, Annalee. Thank you. It means a lot to me." Everyone begins the long process of individual goodbyes, which takes an eternity between eight people. Tristan makes his way to me and it's true that his sweatshirt has several smears of dried paint on it, but one of the shades steals my breath. "That's a very vibrant shade of red, Tristan."

He looks down at his shirt and his mouth falls open. His eyes find his mother's and she jumps in to explain. "It really is. Tristan is constantly covered in paint from whatever project he's working on, and mud from football practice. Tristan." Annalee turns to him. "Next time you must show Emily your latest piece."

He nods, his expression strange and made of stone, "Of course, Mom."

Annalee moves to hug me goodbye, and thoughts about Tristan's sweatshirt consume me the entire way home.

22

EMILY
Saturday, August 7, 2021

Sleep eluded me last night and I ended up falling down the same hole that took me years to climb out of. Suddenly I'm thrust back into the worst moments of my life because I know—I *know*—the proof I need, my salvation, is here somewhere. Jeremey's face pops up in my mind again, smirking at me, dripping with arrogance. Trapping me in its snare. I'm transported back to Moore Road and if I squint, Jeremey's face just fills in the blurry features of the boy only I could see. The feeling settled into my bones at the soccer arena yesterday while Jeremey stared back at me, like he could see right through me. But I must tread lightly. I've been here before. No one believed me then and as it stands, no one would believe me now. But I can't ignore the pit opening in my gut and the new fear that grips me of Harley somehow being connected to this boy.

I can't remove the frayed edges from my thoughts. I gnaw on them, rolling them into a ball and then rolling it around in my mind because there's nothing tangible in this house. I've looked.

The court records and transcripts are with Bryce somewhere, or in a storage unit. Not that I need them, I can replay the entire trial from memory in detail. Then again, after all this time, maybe my brain discarded pieces of this puzzle that a fresh look can decipher. Lincoln is a small town but surely they must archive their content, hopefully digitally to lighten the search effort. I add that to my plate to weed through today.

That leaves me with Harley. I can't stop seeing the look on her face when Jeremey first appeared at her soccer practice, and I can't stop hearing her talk to Theo about it last night like she knew him. Like she's always known him. Does she know him from school? He's older than her. He's the boys' age. My hackles go up at the thought. The friends she talks about from school are all athletes. There aren't many other places Harley might meet people. School, soccer . . . there were lots of families with kids in and out of Lake Harding, but she stayed close to Zola and Annalee's kids. Besides that, Harley has never mentioned another friend in her circle but maybe that is my fault. Maybe the accusations she's hurled at me in the past have some merit and I just wasn't listening to her, or to any of them. I certainly wasn't asking.

I stand outside her bedroom door, where everything is fine. Where I don't know what I don't know. Where I can go on pretending that there's nothing to be concerned about. I thought I knew everything about my daughter. But after last night, it frightens me to think I might be wrong. That I don't know if, or what, she's been hiding. Snooping is a direct breach of trust and I know that when I cross the line, there will be no more pretending that everything is fine. I tried not to dwell on it but the thought that Harley may possibly be Jeremey's next target isn't something I can ignore.

Pausing at the threshold, I gnaw on the idea of violating

Harley's space and privacy, weighing out the consequences. At best, I might learn something Harley's been hiding from me. Or would that be at worst? On the other hand, maybe she's hiding nothing and I'm no closer to proving who Jeremey is, all the while sacrificing my daughter's trust in me by riffling through her personal belongings. Neither outcome is ideal but I justify my decision to snoop by reminding myself that it's my job to protect her from older boys who have a history of trouble. Boys who sneer and make my hairs stand on end.

My time is limited since Harley will be home soon from helping Annalee with the summer book sale at the local library, so I push the door open and step over that invisible line of trust that separates her room from the rest of our house.

I don't have the slightest idea where to start. I check all the typical hiding spots—under the mattress, in her sock drawer, behind the mirror, inside her jewelry box—knowing that Harley is too smart to use any of them. Still, maybe it will give me some momentum. I go to her closet next. Harley packed most of her belongings herself, so I never knew what went into the boxes, or what came out. I drag a couple of boxes out and pull back the flaps.

The first box looks like a bomb went off inside it and it's no great wonder that Harley hasn't unpacked this. Most of this is probably junk. I pluck out a pair of old soccer cleats that I don't think have any sentimental value other than a year's worth of mud and athlete's foot congealed on them. Beneath them is a decorative box and I open it up to find tons of makeup items entirely unopened. I'd always wondered what happened to these. Though she'd long outgrown the makeup phase from her childhood, her friends would give her all the typical girlie favorites for her birthdays without noticing that Harley had never really shown any interest in those things. I keep digging and yank on the corner of a wadded-up T-shirt. It flies out, sending the model airplane that was tucked protectively within its fabric soaring. The airplane's wing brakes with a loud snap when it hits the wall behind me. I pick up the pieces and when my fingers touch the delicate painted wood, I see Ryan again, flying the airplane around his room until the propeller cracked. He never played with it again after that, but I caught him regularly staring at it and running a gentle finger over the crooked left wing that wasn't glued properly during the build. I clutch the pieces to my chest and close my eyes. Harley was always sneaking into his room to play with the airplane like her big brother used to, and I thought Ryan had gotten rid of it when he outgrew it. I had no idea that he'd given it to his sister. That's one secret Harley's kept from me. Why she'd hide something this special I'm not sure, but if she's willing to keep a toy hidden from me, I wonder what else she's locked away somewhere. I set the pieces on Harley's nightstand so I don't forget to talk to her about it.

The next box nearest to me after the disaster I just went through moves easily. When I pull back the flaps, I'm met with more boxes. Stacks of shoeboxes inside one larger moving box. I grab the top box and discover another pair of cleats Harley grew out of long ago. Only Harley would know the logic between putting some pairs neatly in their boxes and tossing one pair into another box with no related items. I close the shoebox and set it to the side, repeating the song and dance twice more before I resort to simply shaking the boxes and listening for the sound of soccer gear. One box towards the middle of the stacks halts my process. It feels empty and weightless. I shake it and a soft rustle comes from inside.

When I open the box, a tiny noise catches in my throat. I plunge my hand into the box to sift through its contents as a tear rolls down my cheek. I tip the box upside down over Harley's bed, dumping out the papers I found inside. Spreading them across her comforter, I'm stunned at how I could have gotten it all so wrong.

23

HARLEY

The state of my bedroom is a different kind of chaos than the carefully curated mess I like to maintain. My shoes suddenly feel like they're full of rocks, making movement nearly impossible.

"Harley, what is all of this?" Mom hovers next to my bed. Her voice is raw, but firm, nothing like the day she told me about how she hit Ryan with her car, when she was eerily calm as if she were telling me any old story. She didn't want to talk then. Today, she wants answers, and I want to hightail it out of here because I know this is going to turn into one of Mom's *chats*, the kind I like to prepare for, but I can tell by her tone that I'm not getting out of this one.

I think she forgets that I know how to play offense. Strike first, strike hard.

"You went through my personal things?" I accuse her, leveling a deadly glare in her direction, and folding my arms across my chest for good measure.

I'm ready for her to explode, but she doesn't. Instead, I watch as she seems to consider her words. Her hands float up to rest on her hips. "You've been keeping secrets from me, about very important things no less." She's using the voice she saves for when she wants to yell but she's trying so hard not to. I can't tell if she's mad because I hid this from her or if she's mad because I know what she's been hiding. Either way, I don't really care.

I snort. "That's rich coming from you."

"Harley . . ." My mom's voice is warning me not to go there with her, but that's exactly what I intend to do. Strike first, strike hard.

"What?" I ask sweetly, feigning innocence. She's losing her patience. Good.

Her hands fall to her sides. "You've been collecting information for God-only-knows how long. When you lie to me like this, I lose trust in you. It makes me wonder what else you're lying about." That's when I see it. The model airplane lying on the nightstand behind her, broken. The body of the airplane still looks intact. I need to keep it that way so Mom doesn't find the pictures hidden inside. At least not until I can figure out what to do about Jeremey.

"Apparently, you already didn't trust me or else you wouldn't have totally violated my privacy like this!" I actually didn't mean to yell. It just happened. Maybe I'm still angry about everything she kept from me, always treating me like a baby. "Besides"—I try again—"you've been lying to me for practically my whole life, about my own brother."

Mom pushes some of the articles to the side and sits down. When she asks me to come sit with her, her voice trembles. I walk over to her, stealing a closer look at the airplane next to her. I plop down on the bed, trying not to draw any attention to the nightstand. My gaze fixes on my hands and I pick at a chip in my hunter-green nail polish, destroying it beyond repair. I'll have to strip it and start all over. Maybe Mom will help me. She has the patience to do them right so that they last.

"Honey, I'm sorry." I can't hide my shock at Mom's apology. I shrug one shoulder. "Whatever."

"No. I was wrong." She sniffles. "I should have talked to you about your brother. About what happened, about who he was and how much I miss him. Every single day." Her hand reaches for mine and clutches it tightly. "I thought I was protecting you from all of this, but I see now that I couldn't. You should have heard it all from me. Instead, I left you to try to put all the pieces together on your own."

I'm not totally sure what to say to that, so I keep it simple. "True."

Mom's thumb moves back and forth over the back of my hand and she chuckles. "A lot of good it did me anyway. Look at all of this. You always were incredibly resourceful." She leans forward to catch my eye and smiles. "Do you remember that summer the boys decided to do a board game tournament, but they wouldn't let you or Theo play? Somehow, they managed to be missing a key piece to every game and you cut them a deal. You offered to help them look, but if you found the pieces, then you and Theo got to play. You were the best little finder on the West Coast."

I look back at the articles I've collected at the library ever since someone graffitied our front door and pluck one from the mess. I turn it over in my hand and skim the words that I remember by heart.

"Ryan Sutton was just the kindest boy you ever did meet," Doris Nedley told reporters. "He wasn't like the other boys paying no mind to an old lady like me. Ryan always said hello when he passed by and asked after my sweet Furcival. This is just such a tragedy and I hope his family makes it through this."

In my memory, I can see the three of us walking down Main Street to pop into Brood for a scone. Ryan would often fall behind,

THE TURN

talking to old Mrs. Nedley or his teacher, Miss Kay, or whoever else we happened to run into. When we got far enough away, Mom would have to call him to catch up. "I didn't just keep the stuff that talked about the trial. Mostly just the stuff that had nice things people were saying about him. When we moved back, I wanted to remember him. Then after the door got painted . . . I just had to know."

Mom stands up, looking resolved. "Let's talk about Ryan more. Deal?" I nod. "And no more lying to each other, right?" I agree, hoping that we both can.

I sigh and my lips part. "What made you go through my room in the first place?" I need to know where I slipped up so that it doesn't happen again.

"I overheard you and Theo talking last night while I was in the bathroom. The window was open." Her head tilts to the side. "Is there anything else you want to tell me, Hart? Something about Jeremey?"

"Not sure what you mean," I reply quickly. Was it too quick? My eyes fly to the airplane without my consent. *Shit.* I whip them back to find my mom eyeing the plane now too. She bends down to pick it up, turning it over in her hands, while her eyes bore into mine. Does she hear my heart pounding? Am I sweating or am I imagining it? Can she feel something loose inside the cargo area? Are the edges of the photos scraping the insides?

"I heard you and Theo talking about Jeremey. It almost sounded like you knew him."

"I do know him. So do you. We met him together, remember?"

Mom's eyebrows fold together and two lines look back at me, considering. "It sounded like maybe you knew him before that." I can't rip my eyes away from the broken plane in her hands. "Harley?"

I snap my focus back in place. "How would I know him before

that if you don't also already know him?" She seems even more thoughtful at that. Did I say something wrong? It wasn't technically a lie. More of a diversion. Logically, it makes sense but she doesn't look any calmer. If anything, it looks like she latched onto something that I can't see. I'm about to say something more but she speaks first, looking down at the model airplane.

"Sorry about this. It fell out of one of the boxes when I was going through it. I'll fix it for you."

I reach for it, freeing it from her hands. "Don't worry about it. I can do that myself." My tongue turns to sand as she continues to watch me. She knows. She must. I need to relax.

"I had no idea you had this. I thought Ryan threw it out," she says, passing the toy back to me. "Why didn't you tell me?"

"I was never allowed to play with it. I was afraid you'd take it away from me." I clutch the toy close to me.

Mom finally seems too tired to continue whatever this standoff is, and she makes her way to the door, stopping only to tell me that she loves me.

When she disappears down the hall, I check to make sure she's gone before I close the door and open the plane up. I look to make sure the photos are still rolled up inside before gently sliding them out.

The photo of us goofing around is still on top, right where I left it. Tristan and Beck are wrestling in the back while Theo and I sit sandwiched between Ryan and Charlie. And there in the distance is the boy with the curls, sitting on the dock, face obscured by the shadows. A second photo sits behind that. Theo and I stand knee deep in the water watching Ryan launch himself from the tire swing while Charlie, Beck and Tristan look on, cheering wildly. On the porch of the cabin next door, the outline of a boy stands watching us. The Moms never noticed him in all those summers. But we did.

THE TURN

The last picture is a close-up of us. Ryan, Charlie, Beck and Tristan have their arms wrapped around me, and Theo, and each other. We wear our biggest smiles, the ones that border on cartoonish. Except this time, the seventh boy is nowhere to be found.

We promised each other no more lies, but Mom didn't mention the articles on my bed that showcased her claims that there was another boy there that day who pushed Ryan into the road. So I pulled that bit of information in close, not willing to admit that I'm beginning to wonder if my mom was right.

It would explain so much.

24

EMILY
Tuesday, August 10, 2021

We step inside the gym and see Raina juggling a soccer ball across the turf while Sawyer checks her form. Sawyer glances over at us and the mood shifts. Though I wouldn't consider myself an empath by any means, I've always been acutely aware of a particular mood when it fills a room. I can feel when someone is sad, pulled down by the weight of it. Or maybe my grief is simply seeking comradery without my knowledge.

I clutch Harley's hand and we walk closer to the turf. I'm not sure how much longer she'll let me hold her hand like this. Right on cue, she drops my hand. My skin tingles and I look up to find Sawyer gazing back at me.

Raina skips over to say hello to Harley. "Oh em gee, Hart! I love your nails! That color is gorg."

"Thanks," Harley replies. "Mom painted them for me." A lump forms at the sound of Harley's pride and she must notice because when I glance down at her, her cheeks burst with pops of crimson. My heart swells at the tiny acknowledgement. It shouldn't matter as much as it does but it feels like affirmation that despite my numerous shortcomings, I'm doing alright as a mother. At least at this one thing.

Raina's smile sags. "I wish someone would paint my nails like this."

I hook a gentle finger under Raina's chin and draw her face up to mine. "Hey, will you be here next week? If you don't mind sitting out one week while Harley does her lesson, I'd be happy to paint your nails, too."

"Really?" Raina lights up.

"Of course! Consider it a *thank you* for letting us hog an hour of your dad's attention every week."

Sawyer approaches and Raina glances at him quickly before returning to me. "That would be awesome! My dad tried once and he ended up painting my whole finger."

Sawyer shrugs. "I did my best."

Raina rolls her eyes while Harley finds a place to put her water bottle down before changing out of her sandals and into her cleats. "I wish you could be around all the time." Raina steps closer to me as if we're in cahoots. "Between you and me, my dad could use a woman's touch."

"Raina!" Sawyer snaps his fingers and narrows his gaze in his daughter's direction.

Raina ignores him entirely and leans in closer. "Are you dating anyone?"

A laugh catches in my nose, creating a half-snort and my hand flies up to cover my mouth. I meet Sawyer's eyes. "Oh, I'm sure your dad doesn't have any trouble finding dates if he's interested."

"Raina, that's enough." Sawyer's voice puts an end to the

discussion, but only just before Raina goes skipping off, arm looping through Harley's, to go warm-up. "Sorry, dad." Raina tosses it casually over her shoulder, sounding not the least bit apologetic.

Sawyer turns to face me. "Sorry about that. Lately, she's a little preoccupied with the idea me dating again." He rubs a hand across the back of his neck. "She thinks I'm lonely. Really, I think she'd just like me out of her hair a little more often."

"She's a fourteen-year-old girl," I muse. "I can certainly understand that."

Sawyer nods. "Well, I better get to it before they hatch some kind of plan."

He turns to go and against my better judgement, I call out, "I'm not, by the way."

Sawyer looks back over his shoulder. "Not what?"

"Not seeing anyone." I half-heartedly shrug one shoulder.

Sawyer looks pained and I know instantly that I've read this all wrong. His signals, our flirtations. God, I'm such an idiot. He was just being friendly, just having fun. "I can't . . . I just don't think it'd be a good idea. Mixing work with my personal life, I mean."

My skin heats up again and I force what I hope to be a casual smile. "Of course not." I leave to find a seat while Sawyer and Harley get to work and pull out my phone to check my work emails.

The hour flies by, likely due to the efforts I take to keep myself distracted from being utterly humiliated. Though every few minutes, I glance up to find Sawyer huddled up with the girls, whose faces, glowing with a light sheen of sweat, are focused on what he's telling them. When they break the huddle, smiles stretch across their faces making my heart flutter over the way he works with them, full of care and enthusiasm. When the lesson ends, all three of them make their way across the turf and I stand to meet them halfway.

"You looked great out there, girls. I feel like you improve leaps and bounds every time."

Harley leans into me and rolls her eyes, this time in jest. "Well, that's the idea, Mom." Raina clamps a hand to her mouth, probably to muffle the giggle threatening to escape.

I look to Sawyer. "Hey, school is starting soon and the regular season too. I know we said we'd scale back, but this seems to be such a good match for Harley." I pause looking at Harley and Raina as they take a couple steps away from us to whisper secrets to each other. "Can we just keep you until you fire us?"

Sawyer snorts, probably as embarrassed by my pathetic begging as I am. "Yeah, that's not gonna happen."

I stammer over my words, trying to find an excuse to mask my embarrassment. "Oh, of course. I know you probably have tons of other players to help and you're probably too busy—" Sawyer stops me before I can bury myself any deeper.

"I meant I'm not going to fire you." I look up, meeting his eyes and he shrugs as he stuffs his hands into his pockets, looking helpless. "Em, I'd never do that. I couldn't." The slight pause between sentences sends a flutter through my stomach and I smother it before my imagination can run away again, with ideas of feelings that aren't there. A harmless little crush is one thing. Reading into it is another thing entirely. A very risky and idiotic thing.

I chew on the inside of my cheek as I try to translate Sawyer's meaning while I search for a reply—any reply—but my thoughts are disrupted by the slamming of the arena doors. We all turn to find Jeremey sauntering through the entrance.

"Jeremey!" Sawyer calls out. "Come over here!"

Jeremey continues over, unhurried. I watch as he approaches, wondering if my mind ran in the wrong direction the other day, seeing what it wanted to see. But Jeremey makes eye contact with me, the same taunting smirk painted on his face, and I can't ignore the alarm blaring inside my mind.

"Jeremey, this is Emily," Sawyer says, clasping his hands together in front of him before turning to Harley. "And this is her daughter, Harley. She's one of my soccer students."

I extend a hand, but Jeremey doesn't return the gesture. I wonder if he'll respond if I speak directly to him. "It's nice to meet you, Jeremey."

Jeremey's eyes darken and he smiles, though his expression is cold. "Yeah. I already know you." My heart freezes inside my chest. I didn't imagine what I saw last week. Instinct demands that I scream at him and force him to admit the truth of who he is. But then, what if I'm wrong? I could destroy everything we've begun to rebuild in the blink of an eye. Besides, I have no more proof now than I ever have.

"I'm sorry, have we met?" I ask coolly, cocking my head to one side, daring him to confirm my suspicions. Part of me feels certain, but as it stands, I'm not—I only have a hunch.

"Yeah, yeah." Jeremey becomes more animated, downright excited. "I definitely know you. You're that lady who killed her own son, right?"

Sawyer's voice rings out and the girls stop, mouths agape. "Jeremey! How could you say that? What the hell is the matter with you?" Suddenly my vision goes blurry and everything around me goes dark.

25

EMILY

When my vision clears, I can hear Sawyer and Jeremey arguing while the girls stand clear of the two of them.

"What? It's fucking true!" Jeremey shouts.

Sawyer steps closer to him. "You have no idea what you're talking about."

Jeremey turns his face away from Sawyer and looks at the ground, lowering his voice. "I read it in the papers. It's all over this podunk town. I saw a picture of her and recognized her from last week. The story is all there."

Sawyer takes a breath before speaking again, his expression unreadable. I can only imagine what he must think of me right now, but he turns back to Jeremey. "I don't care what you think you read. You can't walk around throwing out accusations like that. You're angry, and I get it. You don't want to be here? That's fine. But you don't get to unload your shit on other people. Especially someone you just met. Honestly, the disrespect . . ." Jeremey rolls his eyes and moves to walk away, but Sawyer grabs his shoulders, holding him in place. "I'm not finished. You will get your act together, or you'll be wherever your mom decides to put you next." Jeremey's eyes fall to the ground and what looks like remorse flickers across his face. Sawyer leans in closer to him. "I don't want that for you, but you've got to meet me halfway here," he says softly before releasing Jeremey. "Now, you owe Emily an apology."

Jeremey sighs, seeming to consider Sawyer's words. He turns to me and paints a bright smile on his face. "Right. Sorry about that Emily. I must have been off my fucking rocker." He spins on his heel and makes his way to leave the arena. "I'll wait by the car!" He calls over his shoulder without looking back.

Sawyer releases a long breath before turning back to me. "Em, I am so sorry about that. I don't know what's got into him."

The whole outburst has me rattled and I'm not sure what to make of it. Maybe Harley had a point. I should have told Sawyer what happened. I can't imagine how horrible he is going to feel when he finds out that Jeremey was actually telling the truth, even if he was being a callous little asshole about it.

"It's fine, Sawyer. Really."

"No, he was completely out of line. I'm not sure what he could have possibly been thinking."

Sawyer's apology only makes me feel worse. His blind support of me is something I've craved for years, but I don't want it from someone who doesn't know the whole truth. As usual, I'm making a bigger mess of things by ignoring the issues in the first place. I want to be done with this conversation. I'm not sure what to say so I settle on doubling down on telling Sawyer not to worry about it. "Honestly, Sawyer, please stop. He wasn't—"

"He's just going through a lot. He's a good kid, really. But a while back, he lost his best friend after a horrible accident and he started acting out constantly. He was getting in trouble at school, running away, vandalizing other people's property, stealing . . . His dad isn't around all that much, and Landry hasn't figured out what to do with him. So, she sent him to me which was a colossal mistake, since I don't have the first clue how to handle any of this."

Do I have it all wrong? Maternal instinct swells inside and I can't help but feel a shred of empathy for Jeremey. Sawyer hasn't given me much to go on, but as a mother who has lost one of the most important people in her entire life, my heart aches for this kid who's experienced the same, and seemingly without a lot of support, unlike Tristan, Charlie, and Beck. The urge to protect the broken boy is quickly replaced when I look at Harley. Sawyer may not know what Jeremey has done.

But I do.

I need to remind myself that Jeremey is capable of far worse than sarcasm and a rebellious attitude.

This new information is overwhelming. I have so many questions but it's none of my business, and Sawyer doesn't explain any further. Sawyer looks miserable and I want him to feel better. I could tell him my story now. I could tell him everything, but thoughts of Harley make me waiver. Sawyer might not be phased at all, but if he is, Harley could ultimately end up paying for it. I can't do that to her. I won't.

I look at her face. Something in her expression is curious, waiting to see what I'm going to do with all of this. Her eyes are open wide and her lips part. Maybe it's my imagination but I swear I see her nod, a gentle nudge to confess. To see what happens.

I turn back to Sawyer. "The thing is, Sawyer, Jeremey isn't wrong."

"I'm sorry?"

The room smells of scalding hot asphalt and the overhead lights are blinding. "He wasn't lying. I did kill my son. It's the reason we moved away five years ago."

I don't know why I say it this way, maybe just to see how he'll react to the worst possible version of events. If this doesn't completely scare him off, then maybe he'll be willing to hear me out. Maybe someone will finally understand.

Sawyer's mouth is agape, and he looks to Harley, who suddenly appears sad, then to his daughter who looks as stunned as he does. His eyes whip up to my own and he takes a small step backwards, as if he's afraid he'll be my next victim. As if I could take him without the element of surprise.

"Em?" His voice sounds timid, begging for an explanation. I've done it. I've given him the darkest secret I carry. The one I'll never be able to unburden myself with. And it pushed him too far. He can't handle this about me. That I'm the reason my son is dead. At least it can end with that. I won't have to explain myself to him. This was enough.

"Yes?" I ask softly, standing tall.

He's about to say something when Harley steps forward. "It was an accident!" She sounds breathless as we both turn toward her. I level a gaze at her letting her know I'm not thrilled with her interference. "What? It's true! And I'm not going to stand here and let Coach think you're some psycho killer." Harley folds her arms across her chest and Raina steps forward draping an arm around her shoulders.

The doors to the arena slam back open and Jeremey reappears. "Are you coming, or should I start walking?"

Sawyer doesn't look at him. Instead, he looks me in the eye

THE TURN

and asks, "Can I call you later?"

    I nod and Harley seems to sense that it's time for us to go too. She turns and wraps Raina in a hug and then marches up to me. I put a gentle hand on her shoulder, and we exit the arena together. As we approach the doors, I feel Jeremey's eyes following us. When I look down at Harley, her eyes are glued to the floor, and they stay there until we make it outside where I hear a voice call out. "It was nice to see you again, Emily!" I turn back around to find Jeremey kicking one leg out in front of him as if he's trying to topple something over. A chill runs over me though it's nearly one hundred degrees outside.

26

JEREMEY

Of course, I know who she is. I knew the second I saw her again last week, but I had to be sure whether or not she knew me too. I probably should have played it cool and pretended I had no clue who she was, but my impulsiveness got the best of me. I couldn't resist that opportunity to play with her. Wonder how far she can bend before she snaps. She deserves it after what she did to me. I was just a kid back then. If she's really back here for good, I'm going to have to be careful. I'm not sure what her plan is yet, and I can't afford to make any mistakes. She can't ever know the truth.

27

EMILY

Zola finally picks up on the third ring. "Emily, how are you?"

"Oh, you know, I'm doing fine. You?"

"I'm good! Gotta say, it's weird getting calls from you again. I had this major case of déjà vu and now it's been years. This might take some getting used to." Zola sounds nervous as she laughs on the other end of the phone.

"I know what you mean." I trip over my words a little bit, unsure of how to create a smooth transition. "Look, I'm going to cut to the chase. I promise we'll catch up again soon, but I need a favor."

"Of course, what's going on?"

"You know a cop, right? Didn't you have a connection to a police officer years back? When everything was happening at Bronswood?"

"Oh sure! Josh Pierce. He married into Heather's family." Zola waits a minute before continuing. "Wait, Em? What's going on? Are you in trouble?"

"No, no nothing like that. But I need to look into someone and I need to do it kind of quietly. It's probably not allowed per se, because the person I need information about is a juvenile."

"Alright, you're going to need to give me a lot more than that if you want me to ask my friend to open a minor's records for me."

I explain about Sawyer's nephew. I tell her what I can, leaving out the part about him murdering Ryan. But I tell her how troubled he is and how worried I am about having him around Harley regularly. Zola tells me she understands.

"I'll call Josh as soon as we hang up and let you know as soon as he has anything for me."

"Thank you, Zola. I know it's a big ask and I appreciate your help."

"You're my best friend. I'd do anything for you, Em. Talk to you soon."

"Alright, bye." I disconnect the call and drum nervously on the kitchen table, as if the speed of my fingers will make Zola call me back faster.

I return to my computer and try to focus on the work in front of me but it's no use. My mind wanders. After a respectable thirty minutes of effort, I stand up to pour myself a glass of water and the phone rings, lighting up with Sawyer's name on my screen. I've been on the fence about how much to tell him about what happened to Ryan, but I resolve to tell him as much as I can. Partly because he can simply type a search into Google, and I don't want to do to him what I did to Harley. Look how well that turned out. But a bigger part of me feels like Sawyer might understand. Like he might really see me in all of this.

I hit the button to connect the call. "Hey, Sawyer."

"Em! Hey . . . how are you?"

This is awkward. I hate that it's awkward. "Would you feel better if I said I was fine?"

Sawyer clears his throat and shifts tactics. "Sorry it took me so long to call. I meant to call last night but things just got a little dicey with Jeremey and I was spent."

"What's going on with Jeremey?"

"He's just . . . challenging and I'm in way over my head here. He swings wildly from being angry at everything to not caring about a single thing. He's either popping off with some smart-ass comment or he's pretending like I don't exist or have any say in how he lives his life, even though he's living under my roof, rent free no less."

I try to stifle a laugh, but it slips out anyway. "Sorry! I'm so sorry. It just that, I know you said he's going through a lot, but it sounds like he's a typical teenager."

"Raina isn't even close to this temperamental, and I bet Harley isn't either. I can't imagine her being this hostile."

"Oh, she has her moments, believe me." I flop into a chair nearby. "Give Raina time, she'll get there. Not sure if that makes you feel better or worse about Jeremey."

"Worse. Definitely makes me feel worse." Sawyer lets out a hearty laugh. "But thanks just the same. It helps just to have a fellow parent to lament to."

"Right. Takes a village and all of that . . ."

"So listen, you don't have to tell me your whole history or anything. I was in shock, but you don't owe me anything and I don't want you to feel like you do."

Relief washes over me as Sawyer gives voice to how I was feeling just minutes ago. "Why's that? Because you already googled me and now you know everything?" I joke. God, it feels good to joke. Something about Sawyer puts me at ease. I wait for his response, but his silence confirms that's exactly what he did.

"I'd rather hear your side. Besides, none of the snippets I read tells me what that must have been like for you."

"Alright . . ." I tell him everything. I tell him how I was driving home as the sun was setting. I tell him the way the sun pierced my windshield just as a group of boys appeared on bicycles around the bend. I tell him the way my heart stopped and the world disappeared as I raced to get to the boy pinned beneath his crushed bicycle and peered into the face that I knew better than my own. The face that I made.

I'm crying by the time I finish, though Sawyer doesn't know that soundless tears flow in a steady race down my cheeks as they cleanse the dust from the top of the burden I've carried.

Sawyer's been quiet until now. Listening patiently. "Jesus, Em. I'm not sure what to say here. I am so sorry this happened to you and Harley. How did this ever make it into a courthouse? How could anyone think this was anything other than a tragic accident?"

I swallow, tasting salt from the tears that seeped into my mouth. "A couple of days after Ryan passed, it was like I came out of a trance. I remembered so clearly that it wasn't an accident. That Ryan was pushed into the road."

"What? He was pushed? By who?"

"He was riding with three of his closest friends, boys he'd known for years. But there was a fourth boy riding with them. One I didn't recognize. It all happened so fast, Sawyer." I'm nearly sobbing now, trying to choke down the sound of my lungs gasping for air. "I saw the leg jut out and then the sounds of the metal crunching and then the screams."

"What happened, Em? Where is the fourth boy? I never found any information about him."

THE TURN

I sniffle and drag my nose across the back of my sleeve. "That's the thing. When I told the police about it, they opened an investigation but it didn't take long before they threw in the towel. The other boys, kids I've known for years, who grew up alongside Ryan, told authorities that there was no other boy. Only the four of them. A week later, one of the boys, Tristan, said that he saw me swerve to the edge of the road, like I was aiming for Ryan on purpose. And I did swerve, the skid marks showed that, but I swerved away from them. The town started talking anyway and they thought that I made up the other boy to draw attention away from myself. Either because I didn't want to be convicted, or because I couldn't process the fact that it was my own fault." I take a deep breath of air to steady myself. "It became so much more and eventually, I was charged and taken to court."

"The other boys never confessed? If there truly was another kid who pushed Ryan into the road, why wouldn't they want justice for their friend?" Sawyer sounds agitated.

I shake my head, though I'm alone in the room. "I don't know. Each of the boys testified that I swerved to hit Ryan, which the physical evidence refuted. And none confirmed my testimony that there was a fifth boy present." I don't tell Sawyer that each time I see Jeremey, it increasingly brings the memory of that boy's blurry face into focus, and the mere thought of him stokes the cinders of anger that were reduced to smoldering just moments ago. "I don't blame the boys anymore. I mean, I did. For a long time I was so angry. But after years of therapy, discussions about different trauma responses, and the reliability rates of witnesses, especially young witnesses, I started to understand. They'd just lost one of their best friends. They saw him get hit by a car and they were scared and confused. They were just kids. In the end, two of the boys weren't within sight of the collision anyway. I had to let go of that. I couldn't find any reason they'd set out to hurt me like that on purpose."

"But that can't make you feel any better about losing your son."

"No, it doesn't."

We talk a while longer before Sawyer asks if I want him to come over. As a friend, he clarifies. I tell him that's alright, Harley will be back soon from her run.

I hang up the call and turn over the hazy memory in my mind for the thousandth time. I add Jeremey's face to the mixture and while it seems out of place, with him being so much older now, I can't deny that there's a resemblance. Is it possible that I made up that boy to save myself? Thousands of hours of therapy couldn't bring that idea to actualization. I always thought that I couldn't trust anyone else in this town, but what if it's not them that I can't trust? What if it's me?

28

HARLEY
Wednesday, August 11, 2021

My phone rings nearly two full minutes before I hit the six-mile mark. *Damn it.* Raina is so much faster than I am. It was her idea that we should run together, but since we can't always meet up in person, we share our running app and start our runs at the same time, call each other on our cooldowns. I call her back when I finish the six miles and she is too perky for having run for an hour.

"There you are, slowpoke!" Raina giggles, sounding not the least bit out of breath.

"I wasn't *that* far behind you." I argue, trying not to sound as winded as I feel.

"Who were you listening to today? Maybe it's time to change up your music," Raina muses.

"Avril Lavigne."

"Who's that?"

"Some old-school, punk chick my mom used to listen to a thousand years ago." I chuckle at the image of my mom rocking out to these songs. "She's pretty good, actually."

I hear Raina's hesitation on the other end of the phone before she starts talking again. "So, how are you doing after the whole Jeremey accusing your mom of murder thing? Are you alright?"

Mom and I didn't talk about any of it on our way home, which was great because I definitely didn't *want* to talk to her about it. I couldn't. But I had to talk to someone, so I called Theo last night and told her everything. She couldn't believe it. Last week at dinner I hadn't realized how loud we were being until we heard the clatter from the bathroom and I saw the window was open. Mom said it was her, and that she overheard us. Now she won't stop bugging me about whether Raina has told me anything about Jeremey. She claims she just wants to see if there is any way she could help Sawyer navigate this whole situation, and she can't do that unless she knows more about what he's dealing with.

"I'm fine. I'm glad it happened. My mom never talks about it and I've been trying to get her to tell Coach so that it didn't turn into this weird thing like it always does, because who doesn't talk about their kid they lost, you know? That's so freaking weird. And my brother was awesome, so we should talk about him."

"Well, if you're glad, then I'm glad too. Still, Jeremey didn't have to be such a dick about it if he knew something." If I strain really hard, I can almost hear Raina roll her eyes.

I concede her point. "True. What's his deal anyway? My mom said he's living with you guys for a while? I know Coach said he was dealing with all that junk but like, what really happened? Where's his dad and why can't Jeremey live with him?"

Raina doesn't say anything for a minute and I wonder if I crossed a line into her personal space too soon. "I don't know my Aunt Landry very well. She was just always busy, and for a while we lived too far apart. I've never met my uncle. Even growing up, I don't remember hearing stories about him."

"Oh really? That sucks. Was it hard knowing you had a cousin you didn't get to grow up with?" I can't imagine that was easy, knowing how amazing it was having my brother and Theo, and even Ryan's friends.

"Meh, it was whatever. I didn't know what I was missing, you know? Anyway, Jeremey told me that his dad is in jail! Can you believe it? I've never known anyone with a parent in jail before. And then his mom has a drug problem so she's like, super ill-equipped to take care of him."

"What? That's insane!" I'm not sure if I believe any of this, but I can't tell that to Raina without also explaining why. The memory of Coach Sawyer's rambling pops in my mind and I settle on playing dumb and pry for more. "And Coach said his best friend died in an accident when he younger?"

"Yeah. I don't know all the details, not sure if Dad knows either. Dad said he started causing trouble at school after that and doing stuff like running away from home for days at a time, trashing public property. Just a lot of that kind of thing so I guess Jeremey's mom just couldn't handle that on top of her own shit."

I nod though I know Raina can't see. "Makes sense I guess." It doesn't, actually. It makes no sense but I can't quite fit together the pieces I do have. There's something more here.

"Anyway, I know he's kind of an asshole but I feel sort of bad for him. Must be hard living with all of that."

"Right." I'm not sure what to make of all this but when I turn onto my street, I tell Raina I've got to go. "Thanks for the run! See you at the game." The call disconnects and I try to catalogue the things I know. The closer I get to the house, the more I find myself wishing I could talk to my mom about all of this, to explain everything, but I know that I can't.

29

EMILY
Saturday, Sept 4, 2021

Harley's first preseason game with her new team is a scorcher. The sun feels every bit the magnificent ball of fire that it is, and you can hear the cicadas buzzing around the field. I watch the sweat pour from Harley's brow during warmups and suddenly, her forty-ounce water bottle looks entirely inadequate. This isn't our first season though, and I know the five-gallon water cooler on the sideline can handle the sixteen-girl roster. Plus, I always bring an extra water bottle in case Harley runs out.

Harley's coach, Stephen Ambrose, observes the opposing team quietly, arms folded across his chest and one fist curled tightly at his chin. Sawyer talks to the girls throughout the warmup though I can't hear what he's telling them from my position beneath the soothing shade on the home team's bleachers. Two sharp chirps from the referee's whistle signals to both sides that it's time to take the field. Coach Ambrose and Sawyer jog to the center of the field where they're briefed by the referees and proceed to shake the hands of the opposing team's coaches before trotting back to prepare their starting lineup.

Team captains make their way to center field where the coin toss takes place, awarding our team the opportunity to start on offense. The captains hustle back to tell the team which side of the field to take and how to line up. Harley looks up to me and pats a quick double beat over her heart, which I return. She's outgrown the part where she'll catch the kiss I blow her way, but she'll still give me the piece that tells me I'm with her where it counts.

Harley jogs out to take her place at right midfield. She'll be pulling double the work in this position but that's the way she likes it. I scan the field assessing where Raina and the other girls are stationed. Raina is playing striker in front of Harley and no doubt this is intentional since the girls have been working so closely together over the summer. Sawyer is likely hoping their connection will translate to the field during game play. My gaze follows my thoughts, trailing over to where Sawyer stands exchanging mutters with Coach Ambrose.

I watch, curious about what they might be discussing—strategy, player skills, things they know about the opponent. Sawyer's eyes flick over his shoulder and find mine. He turns, flashing the full charm of his smile my way. He waves and I can't help but grin back, feeling like a silly little girl with a crush. Nothing can happen between us, Sawyer made that clear, but there's no denying there's something there. An undercurrent of comfort and familiarity, playfulness and attraction. It would be a mistake to get involved in any capacity beyond coach and athlete parent, for so many reasons. Not least of all, that would put Jeremey in my path far more often than I could tolerate, and again, when things inevitably go south, Harley is the one who will be hurt the most. But god, he's hot as hell. I remind myself that it's just a little crush and wave back at him just as Coach Ambrose turns to see who Sawyer is waving at. Sawyer drops his hand like he got caught cheating on a spelling quiz and returns his focus to the field where the referee's whistle has just announced the start of the game.

Sawyer is different during gameplay. The other team is aggressive, and Sawyer spends minute after minute barking orders at our girls, shouting reminders of this drill and of that formation they've memorized during their private lessons. It's mesmerizing to watch the way Harley and Raina fall into rhythm, gravitating to the right place like they're reading each other's mind or speaking a silent language only the two of them understand. Their work with Sawyer is paying off, that much is obvious when he coaches them to the goal and they don't spare a glance to where he stands on the sidelines. Rather, they adjust their positions and feed the ball exactly to the space that he sees in front of them, splitting a pair of defenders with ease, dribbling into an open space, and before anyone has time to retaliate, Sawyer is yelling "cross!" at the exact moment Harley punts the ball into the middle of the box where Raina is poised, waiting with the laces of her right cleat ready to strike. The play is over in the blink of an eye when Raina slams the ball into the back of the net, scoring the first goal of the season. We all cheer and Raina points to her dad on the sideline as she trots back to her starting position.

All throughout the game, Sawyer is focused with absolute attention while the team is in motion, but I feel the glances cast my way during a dead play. The girls huddle up during a timeout and as they break, Sawyer takes a moment to steal another look and I feel my cheeks flame when he grins at me. My eyes drop to my lap out of habit. He said he didn't want to start anything romantic, but the whiplash between his words and his actions is making me feel like

I'm not imagining the spark between us. I wonder if he's changing his rigid stance on keeping work and personal life separate. I'm starting to think I'm ready to break some of my own rules, mainly the one where I don't do romantic relationships.

When I manage to look up, his expression has changed into something else entirely. His smile is gone and, in its place, his brows are pinched tight, his thoughts unreadable. I can't imagine what he might have seen in my face to disappoint him but a moment later I realize that he's no longer looking at me. He's looking just beyond. I sneak a careful look over my shoulder to discover Jeremey seated just a few rows above me. He catches me looking and smirks, tossing a smug salute of his first two fingers in my direction. I turn back to the game without waving at him, just in time to see Sawyer fold his arms across his chest. I doubt I'll be receiving any more flirtations for the rest of the game with Jeremey sitting up there killing any buzz we might be getting.

Zola called a few days after I asked her to dig up some information about Jeremey and I haven't stopped thinking about it. Unfortunately, it didn't result in many specifics. Detective Pierce wasn't able to disclose anything to us as Jeremey is still a minor, but Zola did confirm that Jeremey has quite the rap sheet riddled with things like truancy, petty theft, a few physical altercations at school that grew increasingly more violent over the years. All things point to him being a continued threat. One that I have to handle with care if I want to prove he killed Ryan.

I let out a low sigh before I realize this may be the opportunity I need. A couple weeks ago, Harley came back in from a run and plugged her phone into the charging station while she shuffled off to shower. She and Raina had been texting and Harley left her laptop open on the couch near where I was seated. Their conversation lit up before my eyes and before I knew it, Jeremey's life history was laid out before me. He had a tough upbringing. But that doesn't give him the right to take away my son and then screw with me and my family. Now, Jeremey is alone with no one around to explain away his history or his behavior. I'm curious what he might say to me if he thinks no one else will hear. A deep breath fills my lungs and I stand to march the few steps up to the bench where he's seated.

"Can I sit with you?" I ask, trying to sound relaxed.

Jeremey forces a smile but it doesn't look quite right. "Of course you can, Emily. Be my guest." He sweeps a hand across the bleachers, presenting me with the seat next to him. What I want to do is slap the fake grin off his face. What I actually do is gather my composure and sit.

I turn my face to examine him, searching for the confirmation I no longer need because I feel it deep in my bones—I know this boy. "I think maybe we got off on the wrong foot," I offer. It's one thing to know who Jeremey is. It's another thing entirely to know how to handle him. The anger began boiling in my bones from the moment I saw him but I'll keep my cool. Of all the ways I can approach this, I know losing it on him will get me nothing.

Jeremey keeps his eyes pointed at the field. "Is that right? I suppose you want an apology?"

My blood heats. I underestimated my ability to stay calm. "You're damn right I want an apology. But not for that," I say through gritted teeth.

Jeremey turns his head and his eyes darken. "Hmm, I'm not sure what you're talking about, Em."

A knot forms in my stomach at his use of my nickname. Every fiber inside me is lit, ready to scream the truth, but a part of me knows it would only add more venom to his bite. A more passive path opens up in front of me and I force myself to recalibrate before taking it. "I know that you lost your best friend in a car accident years ago. And you know all too fucking well that's a pain that I understand. Don't you."

His head cocks to the side and I know I've got him cornered. His bites his lips together until they turn white. "What do you really want from me Emily? You're working too hard here. It's embarrassing, honestly. You want me to put in a good word with my uncle? Cause I gotta tell you, I don't have a lot of sway in what he deposits into his spank bank."

It's more than apparent why Sawyer is struggling so much with him. There isn't much worse than a teenage boy who's angry at the world. Except perhaps an angry mother. And this boy has reignited the fire that consumed me six years ago. The anger that simmered beneath the surface for so long as life continued to move forward. Jeremey stands abruptly, just as I'm about to let loose my rage. "If you'll excuse me, I think I'll go call my dad. He's expecting me." He walks off before I have the chance say anything. I watch him walk out to the parking lot and turn my attention back to the game. It only takes a quick scan to see Sawyer staring up at where Jeremey and I were just talking. Sawyer's eyes connect with my own for a moment before he goes back to work and the knot in my gut spools tighter.

The game ends and I make my way down to the field, hating myself for being so distracted from Harley's season opener. I mask the guilt with an abundance of enthusiasm over their win. Harley and Raina walk off to say goodbye to their teammates before gathering their bags, and I turn to find Sawyer approaching me.

"Hey, so, I saw you talking to Jeremey. Everything okay there? Was he giving you any trouble?"

I shake my head. "No," I lie. "Everything is fine." I reach out, pulling Sawyer a few steps away from the others so that I can lower my voice. "I was just trying to make peace and I thought maybe we could relate a little over losing someone important to us. I think it backfired." My eyes fall to the field which I hope Sawyer interprets as remorse. "I'm sorry. I think I upset him. He took off, saying he had to call his dad."

Sawyer's face is tight with anger. He shakes his head. "I'm going to have a talk with him. Just because he's pissed off at everyone doesn't mean he gets to take it out on you—"

I hold up a hand. "Don't be too hard on him. You said it yourself that he's been through a lot. And it must be even harder with his mom struggling with addiction and having to call his dad in prison."

A light flicks on behind Sawyer's eyes. "What did you say?"

I wonder what I said wrong. Was I not supposed to know these details? Maybe they're family secrets. "Oh, I'm sorry. I shouldn't have said anything . . . I won't tell anyone—"

"Landry doesn't have a problem with drugs or alcohol."

"She doesn't?"

"No! I don't think she's ever touched an illegal substance in her entire life. And Jeremey's dad isn't in prison." I watch as a realization seems to dawn on him. "Is that what he told you? Jesus, I could just strangle that kid . . ."

"I just . . . I thought . . . he . . ." I'm unable to form a coherent thought, or even speak a complete sentence. My mind is reeling with this revelation as I gesture blindly in the direction Jeremey went.

"Jeremey's dad is a pilot. Sure, he's not around much but that's because his schedule is hectic. Not because he's in prison."

"He's not? Are you sure?"

Sawyer chuckles awkwardly. "Yes, Em. He's a former Marine but when he was discharged, he became a pilot. We don't hear from him much, but he's not a criminal. Jeremey sees him as much as he can. He's got a place up north."

30

HARLEY

Jeremey and Raina are arguing and I'm not sure whether to let them hash it out or attempt to broker a truce.

"You had no business spreading my personal life all over town, Raina!" Jeremey shouts. "I told you all of that stuff in confidence and now you're screwing everything up."

I thought Raina might step back, but instead she takes a huge step into Jeremey's space and stands tall. "First of all, you never told me that info was private and second, I think you're doing a great job of messing things up all by your dumbass self."

Jeremey rolls his eyes and snorts in disbelief, which only makes Raina push harder. "Seriously! Why are you being such a total asshat to my dad? He took you in and he's just trying to help you after you pushed your mom over the edge."

"If your dad really wanted to help, then where has he been for the last six years, huh?"

"That's not fair. Your mom never told him anything was going on. We tried reaching out but—"

"That's bullshit, Raina. Your dad didn't want you anywhere near me so I wouldn't corrupt you."

The direction their fight is going is making me anxious and I move closer to them, sliding my hands between them to separate them. "Jeremey, come on. Maybe if you just told—"

Jeremey pins me in place with a stare and my voice catches in my throat. "I don't think you want me telling anything to anyone, right, Hart?" He leans in closer to me, angling his mouth away from Raina and into my ear, whispering, "You're not going to break your promise now, are you? You remember what will happen. There's no expiration date, you know?"

I step back and I can see Raina in my periphery, staring, mouth agape. "What are you guys talking about? Harley, do you know something you're not telling me?" I shake my head, eyes never leaving Jeremey's. Before I can respond, I hear shouting coming from behind me. We all turn to see my mom and Coach Sawyer marching over to us. Both of them are yelling at once, making it much less understandable and much more like a garbled mess of sounds.

My mom looks wild as she whips a hand out, grabbing me by the arm and tucking me into her side. She often forgets that I'm not a little kid anymore and I wriggle out of her grasp and stand just beside her. She sets her sights on Jeremey who looks as cool as ever, utterly unbothered. "You told me that your father was in prison," Mom says, accusing him.

Jeremey pulls his head back, looking at my mom like she's lost her mind. "No, I didn't."

"Yes, you did!"

Coach Sawyer steps in. "Jeremey, if you're lying to me, so help me God . . ."

"I didn't!" Jeremey insists, turning his eyes back to my mom. "All I said was that I was going to call my dad. I told Emily he was expecting me, that's all." Jeremey looks back at Coach Sawyer. His eyes look genuinely remorseful and that split-second reminds me how careful I need to be around him. "I was just trying to be polite by not running off in the middle of our conversation, Uncle. It's not my fault if she assumed something worse. I don't even know where she got a crazy idea like that." Coach Sawyer doesn't notice the subtle flick of Jeremey's eyes in Raina's direction, but I do, because I know exactly where the idea came from and I can't believe my mom was snooping again! She promised she wouldn't. Raina is staring at the asphalt beneath her sandals.

Coach looks at my mom, silently asking whether that might be true. I can count the number of times my mom has looked uncertain on one hand. For the first time in a long time, she seems to be questioning herself. It should be one of those things that proves to me that she's human and is capable of making mistakes, but instead, it's making me anxious. I know what lengths my mom will go to in order to prove she's right. The court reports showed as much. Or at the very least, so that others don't see that she's wrong. I was just starting to think she may be right about far more than being wary of Jeremey. But now . . .?

My mom shakes her head gently as if she's replaying whatever happened between her and Jeremey earlier. "No. No, I guess you didn't say that. I . . . I just assumed."

"And what gave you that idea?" Jeremey is daring my mom to throw me and Raina under the bus since he found out Raina told me his secrets. I'm not sure how my mom figured it out, but I guess that doesn't matter much. My mom would never rat us out but luckily, Coach Sawyer intervenes before she has to make up a new lie.

"Lay off, Jeremey." Coach Sawyer pulls him to the side. "She made a mistake. Let's not turn it into something it's not."

"Typical . . ." Jeremey's voice trails off as Coach Sawyer drags him further away. I take the opportunity to pounce on my mom. "Mom, can Raina come over to do homework?" I don't want Raina to have to go home with Jeremey right now. Mom will say yes, if for no other reason than to cover up her embarrassment at what just happened.

I watch my mom force a smile into place. "Of course. Raina, you're always welcome, honey. As long as it's okay with your dad."

Raina smirks at me knowingly. "Oh, I'm sure it will be. My dad never has a problem with me staying at your place. Especially if it means he'll have to come pick me up later." She skips off to ask her dad before Mom can say anything.

Raina returns a moment later, confirming that Coach Sawyer will pick her up in a couple hours and we turn as a group and start walking to the car. I sneak just one glance over my shoulder to find Jeremey watching us go, a silent finger pressed to his lips.

31

JEREMEY

I knew Raina would go blabbing to Harley. She says I can trust her but at the end of the day, she's still a teenage girl. I was surprised at how quickly the gossip made it over to Emily though. I expected more time to go by before Emily came for me.

I'm not surprised my uncle is so whipped for Emily, honestly. I've watched her with Raina, and Sawyer, and especially Hart. She's good at playing nice when she wants. And she's smart, but I'm smarter. I have to be. It's fun to watch her shift tactics so quickly, trying to figure me out. Emily thinks she knows me, and she does. But she doesn't know the half of it. Her blinders are on. I can see the wheels turning in her head. She ruined everything that first summer. And I'm going to make sure she regrets what she did to me.

She doesn't remember yet but I can see that she's trying. It's only a matter of time, but that's fine.

You'd have thought that her son dying would have been punishment enough, but apparently, she wants more. She just can't leave it alone and move on. But she also can't prove it. I made damn sure of that. She couldn't back then, and she won't be able to now.

I wasn't planning to hurt him.

The mention of the car accident was a surprise. I wasn't expecting that, but it doesn't matter. I know Sawyer didn't tell her about it because he didn't know what kind of accident it was that took my best friend from me. Emily showed her hand too soon, and I'm going to make her fold.

32

EMILY
Saturday, Sept 11 2021

I'm nearly ready when Sawyer appears at the front door. To say I was shocked when he called after last week's soccer game to ask me out is an understatement. Between his feelings about mixing business with pleasure and the debacle with Jeremey, I'd have bet the house that dating was not only off the table, but in another zip code entirely. With the girls' overly enthusiastic blessing, Sawyer is here to pick me up for dinner while Raina stays with Harley, bringing with him a slew of flutters deep in my belly. I haven't dated in a couple decades, but something about Sawyer is comforting and familiar. Like we should have done this so long ago and now we're playing catch-up.

The door swings open. "Hi Raina! Come on in. Harley is in the living room."

Raina races past me, dropping a casual "Hey, Ms. S." in her wake.

I look up and Sawyer's eyes lock with mine. "Hey."

"Hey," he replies, taking a step closer to me, pressing deeper into my space. "You look amazing."

I'm wearing dark wash, fitted denim with a flowy tank top, just short enough that a sliver of my stomach peeks out when I lift my arms, but not so short that Harley would accuse me of not dressing my age. "Thanks. You clean up nicely yourself." And he does. His denim hugs him in all the right places and his plain white T-shirt is just the right fit.

Sawyer steps inside and we find the girls huddled on the couch giggling about something. "Alright girls, we'll only be gone for a few hours and I expect the phone to be answered every single time that I call. Understood?" This is the first time I'm leaving Harley home alone with a friend or for more than twenty minutes. It might be overkill but I'm not willing to risk anything happening to her.

"Geez, Mom. We get it. We're not going to throw a kegger while you're gone."

"How do you know what a kegger is?" I ask, and Harley responds with her signature eye roll.

"We promise, Ms. Sutton. We won't cause any trouble," Raina chirps.

I nod just as Sawyer steps forward to hug Raina. "Be good." He probably meant to whisper it but he was loud enough for the whole room to hear.

"Dad, I just said that I would. Chill."

"Alright, alright." Sawyer relents, turning to face me. "Shall we?" I take his hand and we make our way to the door.

"Have her home by ten!" Harley calls out.

"Use protection!" Raina yells.

"Raina Marie!" Sawyer snaps and my hand flies up to my mouth, trapping the laugh behind my lips. The girls are not so subtle and their hysterical laughter follows us out of the house. "I'm so sorry about that . . ." Sawyer stammers.

"Don't be. She's just having fun."

Sawyer doesn't look inclined to let it go but I cut him off before he can argue. "So where are we headed?"

"A fun little spot that I think you'll enjoy." He opens the passenger side door for me, grinning in a way I can't quite interpret, but feels very much like he's savoring the moment as his eyes rove over my body. I flush, ducking my head so I can slide in, and when the door closes, my heart skips a beat. The Sawyer I once knew was just a kid. But this Sawyer is new, and he seems to be fully aware of the effect he has on me.

Old Town Pizza has a rooftop patio that I had no idea existed. But Sawyer knew and I love that he picked a place that is both familiar and well loved, but has something exciting to offer too. He requested a table by the roof's edge so that we can overlook the old, main road through downtown Lincoln.

"I wasn't sure how much pressure you like to put on a first date so I thought this was a good compromise. The food is good, but they also serve at least five different wines if you're feeling fancy."

"This is perfect." I tell him, wondering where my cheeks fall on a scale of blush to cherry tomatoes.

The server comes over to take our order and Sawyer orders a beer while I stick with water. "Are you ready to order food or do you need another minute?"

I look to Sawyer who shrugs, telling me to order for us both.

"I'm ready. We'd like a small Choo Choo Chicken, and add jalapeños please."

"I'll get that right in," says our server as they scamper off to another table.

Sawyer looks as though he's trying not to smile. "What's that look for? Did you want something else?"

"No, no. It's perfect. I'm just marveling at the fact that you skipped the salad and added jalapeños. A woman after my own heart."

I laugh. "Well, let's be honest. A salad never fills me up enough to make a difference in how much pizza I'll eat so what's the point? I feel like it's just for show. And what kinds of psychopaths are you dating who don't like jalapeños?"

The question gets a full belly laugh from Sawyer and it feels like I've won some kind of prize I didn't know I was working for. "Hey now, I haven't dated a psychopath in a long time. Or anyone at all for that matter."

"Mmm." I nod. "And why is that?"

Sawyer seems to consider his response. "Too many red flags, I guess. I see enough of those on the field." He shrugs and we fall into easy conversation, rehashing memories from our time living on the same street, each asking questions about the other's life after that.

"How's your mom doing? I always loved seeing Sarah Beth. She always had something baking and a pitcher of sweet tea! I loved that tea."

"She's good. She had a rough go of things after my dad ran off. He left a financial disaster behind, but you remember my mom. She always figured it out." I nod thoughtfully, remembering well the way I always thought Superwoman's alias must have been Sarah Beth Dennis. "She lives up in Folsom now and she comes to a lot of Raina's games. That's a lot of the reason I never ended up living too far away from where I grew up. I wanted Raina to be close to my mom. She's a fantastic grandma, though it's hard to track her down sometimes. She keeps busy with volunteer work and a hobby baking business. Still a hustler. Can you imagine?"

A tiny snort escapes my nose. "I actually really can." I pause before broaching what I can only assume must be a sensitive subject. "I'd forgotten that your dad took off."

Sawyer waves it away. "That was right after I moved out. I hadn't seen you in a while at that point."

"Still, I saw your mom. I should have checked up on her. Did you ever find out where he went?"

"Nope. It remains a great mystery to this day. It's better that way though. I have nothing to say to him after what he did. I can't imagine any good could come from him showing up." I reach a hand across the table and fold his into my own. "We're all good now." His eyes drag slowly from our hands, up my arm until they're locked on mine. "We're great, actually."

Sawyer rips his hand from mine when the server returns with our food and I have to squelch a strange bite of resentment for our waiter. The feeling subsides as the first taste of tangy white sauce mixed with the heat of the jalapeños hits my tongue. I'd forgotten how delicious this pizza is and an embarrassing moan escapes my lips. I glance up to find Sawyer working hard to suppress a smile as he watches me. He isn't watching me as much as reading me. His eyes travel back and forth over my face like he's attempting to translate each line. "What? It's really good!"

"Yeah, I can tell," he says teasingly. "So, we've learned that jalapeños aren't an issue here. Tell me, any red flags I should know about?"

I bite off a chunk of the crust in my hand and chew it thoughtfully. I toss a devilish look in Sawyer's direction before dunking the crust into the ranch dressing sitting on the table between us. "Well, if the ranch is top tier, I'll double-dip hoping whoever I'm with notices and becomes so grossed out, they give me the rest of it."

Sawyer bursts out laughing. "Any reason you can't simply ask the server to bring you more?"

"And risk being an inconvenience to the person whose exact job it is to bring me the food I ask for?" I feign shock at the suggestion. "Never." I plunge my crust into the ranch again, pointedly watching Sawyer's reaction as he realizes what I'm doing.

He simply smiles and pushes the dish closer to me before dipping his own crust into it. "I don't mind sharing." The moment seems to stretch on before he finally adds, "Any other glaring issues I should know about?"

"Well, it's not applicable tonight because we're eating the exact same thing, but if we're going to keep seeing each other, you should be prepared to factor me into what you order."

"Meaning?"

"I've been known to order one thing and then lust after the other person's meal, requesting tiny tastes until eventually they just relent and give me half their plate while mine grows cold."

"Any red flags that perhaps aren't food related?"

"Does coffee count as food? Because there are several in that department."

We exchange questions between bites. I explain how we came to be in Lincoln after looking for a family-oriented town to raise the kids in when Bryce got relocated to the area. Sawyer answers my prodding into how he became a competitive soccer coach on top of a successful real estate broker. "As Raina became more involved in soccer and her schedule increased, it seemed like the easiest way to spend more time with her. My schedule is flexible and I can take on more work in the offseason, decrease when pre-season ramps up." I'm not sure how to ask but I don't think Sawyer would misjudge my intensions as I venture a little closer to private matters. "Where is Raina's mom?"

Sawyer takes a sip of beer to wash down his food, looking resigned. "It's been me and Raina since she was a baby. I wasn't super responsible around the time my dad left and when I hooked up with Vanessa, she ended up getting pregnant. I didn't handle it very well and she showed up at my door one day when Raina was about nine months old, shoved Raina in my arms and took off. I've tried tracking her down over the years, at Raina's request, but Vanessa's managed to dodge me all this time. She doesn't want to be found." He clears his throat before adding, "I don't think it would do Raina any good to know her though. I'd rather she has the stability of her mother not being here, than to watch the way she floats in and out of her life at a moment's notice, you know? Raina deserves someone she can count on and I work hard to make sure the she knows that's me."

It's hard not to like Sawyer a little more after hearing about how special his relationship with Raina is. My phone rings and I slide it from my bag to make sure it isn't Harley. When I see that it's Bryce, I silence the call and drop the phone back into my purse. "Sorry about that."

Sawyer is utterly unfazed. "You can take it if you need to. I don't mind."

I shake my head. "No, it was just Harley's dad. It's not important." Sawyer asks me what happened between me and Bryce, if I don't mind telling him.

I consider whether I mind or not. It isn't as if I can't talk about Bryce, it's more that I don't want to. Talking about Bryce means that

I have to talk about Ryan, and that's a wound that always feels fresh. But Sawyer opened up to me, I can do the same for him. I'll have to if we want to give whatever this is a fighting chance. "There isn't too much to tell. Our marriage just couldn't weather everything that happened with Ryan. It's pretty common for marriages to crumble under the weight of child loss, but for me, it wasn't that exactly. It was that I never felt like Bryce believed me when I told him that Ryan was pushed. He was never on my side and so I just felt alone in all of it. And when the town seemed to turn on me too . . . Bryce had an affair at the same time and it was just too much. I packed up our stuff, took Harley, and ran." My thoughts wander back to that day when I shut the front door for the last time, without so much as a note. "It wasn't right. I should have handled it differently."

Sawyer reaches for my hand, heat radiating from his skin. "You were just trying to survive it. You were doing what you thought was best for you and Harley." Once again, I'm struck by the feeling that Sawyer sees me at my core, free of judgement.

The moment is ruined by my phone once more. Sawyer releases me to check the caller ID and I find Bryce's name light up the screen. I sigh. "I'm so sorry. I should take this. He does this and he'll just keep calling until I answer." I slide my chair back to stand, walking as close as I can get to the corner where I can pretend like I have any sort of privacy while I take Bryce's call.

"You can't keep doing this, Bryce. Your time isn't more important than mine and you can't just blow up my phone any time you have something you need to unload on me."

"Knock it off, Em. You know damn well that it's the only way I can get your attention. You don't take my calls, and you won't return my messages."

"I'm busy right now, Bryce. What do you want?"

"Oh, I know you're busy. How is Sawyer doing? I didn't realize soccer coaches were in the habit of taking their athletes' mothers out to dinner. Did you have to pay extra for that?"

My blood ignites and I'm dangerously close to making a scene on the roof of Old Town Pizza. I settle for whisper yelling. "You are such an asshole. You have no business telling me what I can do with my free time. How did you know where I was, anyway?"

"I was in the area so I stopped by to see my daughter and I find out that she's home alone with a friend because her mother can't keep it in her pants."

I refuse to let Bryce get to me right now. It's exactly what he wants. "That's rich, Bryce. Really, coming from you."

"What's that supposed to mean?"

"You think if you just keep dropping in and being nice that I'm just going to forgive you and everything will go back to the way it was. But you don't seem to understand that it can't. And I don't want it to. You made your choices. Now I'm making mine and you don't get to just pop in when you're lonely and make me feel guilty for hating you." I spit the words at him through the receiver.

I'm met with silence on the other end of the phone. "You hate me?" Bryce sounds genuinely wounded, like the thought had honestly never occurred to him.

"Goodbye, Bryce. Don't call me again tonight, and you better not be at the house when I get home." I disconnect the call before he can respond and I turn the ringer off before returning to the table to try to salvage what's left of this date. My first thought is that maybe I was too harsh. I don't hate him exactly. Not anymore. Then I realize that I don't care if I hurt his feelings. Bryce made his bed. Actually, he made someone else's. He can lie in it or not. Either way, I'm not responsible for making him feel better.

Though, I'm not sure what I was thinking, trying to get involved with anyone. My life is complicated enough without dragging Sawyer into the mess. Jeremey would be a huge thorn that would continue burrowing its way into my side. I'd have to see him that much more if this went well. Then what if it didn't go well? How would that affect Harley? I haven't the slightest clue how to reconcile any of this to myself, let alone to those who'd be dragged to the middle of the mayhem.

33

EMILY

When Sawyer looks at me, his expression makes it obvious that he overheard everything. "Everything okay?"

I nod and put a smile on my face, hoping it doesn't look half as forced as it feels. We make it through the rest of dinner, but the mood has shifted and when Sawyer asks if I want to call it a night, I'm disappointed. But, I reluctantly agree because I can understand why he would want to tap out. The drive home is quiet and when we pull into the driveway, I see Bryce's car parked on one side. "Damn it." Sawyer looks at me, questioningly. "That's Bryce's car." We climb out of the car and head inside.

Raina and Harley are laughing from the couch and their giggles bring a sense of calm before the storm that's brewing as Bryce stands from where he's seated and marches towards us. I try to move forward to meet him, slogging through tension thick as mud, but Bryce pulls me into a hug with a smile on his face. He looks warm, but his arms feel like ice. "Em, it's so good to see you."

Bryce glances up at Sawyer and smirks knowingly. "I hope you kids had fun." I was right telling Bryce off the way I did. He'll never change. He's trying to make Sawyer feel insignificant but his one-sided dick measuring contest is embarrassing. "Uh, Em. Could I speak to you for a moment? I promise I'll have her back in a blink," he says to Sawyer. Bryce makes his way toward the kitchen before I can protest, and pounces the moment I turn the corner. "What are you doing here, Em?"

"The better question is what are you doing here. I've already told you that you can't just show up anytime you want, Bryce. We aren't married anymore. You don't live here."

"I know that! You've made that incredibly clear. But come on, you can't possibly think it's a good idea for you to mess around with Harley's soccer coach."

I take a steadying breath. "It's none of your damn business who I'm involved with."

Bryce has the nerve to look disappointed in me. "Em. You aren't yourself. You haven't been since you moved back. I think it was a mistake for you to come back."

"How would you know whether I've been the same? You stopped noticing me long before we left."

"I know what you've been up to. You're asking for the old court docs . . ." He says this like it makes his point. Rather than deign to respond, I just wait. Bryce has a need to fill the silence and I know I won't have to wait long for him to continue. "You're digging again, Em! You're unearthing everything we worked so hard to put behind us. I didn't really want you to come back. I wanted to sell the damn house. And look what happened. You were barely here before someone painted murderer across the door and tried to run you out of town."

This revelation stops me in my tracks. "How did you know that?"

"What?"

"How did you know someone painted the door?"

Bryce looks like an animal caught in a trap, scrambling to escape. "I . . . doesn't matter. Harley told me, whatever. The point is nothing good will come from you poking around again. You have to move on."

Harley didn't tell him about the door. I'm sure of that, but that doesn't tell me how he knows. I'm ready to be done with this conversation. I've already given Bryce more time than he deserves and Sawyer is waiting in the hallway. "I have moved on Bryce. I've moved on from you. You need to accept it." I leave the kitchen with Bryce on my heels and Sawyer shoots a half-hearted smile my way and I wonder, once again, how much he overheard.

I send Sawyer an apology with my eyes but he doesn't seem to notice. Instead, he thrusts a hand towards Bryce. "Hey, you must be Bryce. I'm Sawyer, Raina's dad and Harley's soccer coach. Nice to finally meet you." Bryce shakes his hand tentatively while Sawyer continues. "I've heard a lot about you."

Bryce lights up, completely unaware that what Sawyer has heard is nothing good. "Uh huh, and I've heard nothing but great things about you, too."

"I'm happy to hear that." Sawyer shoots me a quick wink before nodding towards the couch where Harley and Raina are peeking over the back watching the showdown with eager eyes. "You've got a great kid over there. Raina and I are big fans." Sawyer shoots a warm smile in the girls' direction and Raina drapes her arm around Harley's shoulders.

"That's my Hart. I couldn't agree more."

I interrupt before things can continue. "Harley, why don't you and Raina clean up and you can say goodnight to your dad."

Bryce heads over to help the girls and Sawyer leans in and whispers in my ear. "Can we talk outside for a minute?" I know what's coming. He's going to let me down gently because he's a great guy, but this was too much. He has to focus on what's best for him and Riana and Bryce isn't best for anyone. I didn't need bliss. I'd have settled for contentment. But god, Sawyer might have been bliss. I follow him out and quietly shut the door behind me.

"Listen, I know—"

Sawyer cuts me off as he spins me around to face him taking both my hands in his. "Hey, this was a lot for you. I can see that. But I had a really good time." He runs lazy circles with his thumbs on the backs of my hands. "Can we try again? I know things are complicated with Bryce, and Jeremey, and two girls in the mix. And I know what I said about mixing business with pleasure. But I just can't help thinking that I'm going to miss out on someone amazing if I let you go."

Before I can say anything, he releases one of my hands and I feel the heat from his palm wind around my waist and press into the small of my back. His other hand grazes gently up my arm, traces my skin up and over my shoulder, then higher up my neck where his palm comes to rest on the side of my face, his thumb hooking under my jaw, eyes never leaving mine. He tilts my face up until he has the angle he wants and he leans in. His lips are soft at first, tentative, as if waiting for my signal. I drag my fingers through his hair as my lips part, inviting him in, and he pulls me against him, deepening his kiss. When his tongue slips in my mouth, I feel it in my stomach and a tiny gasp escapes between us.

Sawyer pulls back just as the front door swings open revealing

Raina with her bag slung over her shoulder. Sawyer drops his hands, but he wasn't fast enough and Raina takes full advantage of the situation. "Am I interrupting something?"

Sawyer ignores her. "Did you say goodbye to Harley?"

"Of course. Thank you for having me over, Ms. S." Raina chuckles, looking smug as can be when she turns to her dad. "Looks like you've already thanked her?" Sawyer gives her a look that sends Raina into a fit of laughter as she skips to their car.

Bryce steps out on to the porch, looking ready to take his parting shot at Sawyer. "It was nice meeting you, Coach. Thanks for taking such good care of my family."

Sawyer doesn't bat an eyelash. He looks at me while he answers Bryce. "Anytime." He smirks and drops his voice as he squeezes my hand one last time. "Goodnight, Em."

I watch them leave and then turn to go inside, telling Bryce he can leave now, before I shut the door, locking him outside.

34

HARLEY
Saturday, October 2, 2021

Friendsgiving. I only remember a couple of them before we moved but they're up there in my favorite memories bank. The moms said it was too hard to host a real Thanksgiving together with three families because of relatives that come to visit, so they made their own holiday that was just for us. We'd all pack up and head to Zola's cottage at Lake Harding where we'd stay for the weekend and prepare a huge meal that we'd eat out on the back deck. Zola always went all-out and everyone picked a favorite dish to bring. It was way too much food and we were packed into the tiny cottage like sardines, but that's the way we liked it.

I can't wait to get up there. I thought it would be awkward seeing everyone after all this time but that first dinner a couple months ago at Annalee's was way more comfortable than I expected. Even though this major and life-altering thing had happened keeping us apart for years, it was like practically no time had passed. This first Friendsgiving back is going to be extra special because Coach Sawyer is joining and bringing Raina with him. Mom danced around the idea for a super long time and finally asked me if I felt alright with her inviting them, saying that she understood that they might be moving fast, then quickly explained that away by reminding me that she's actually known Sawyer for practically her whole life and blah blah blah. I can't seem to get her to understand that I don't mind. I haven't seen her this happy since before Ryan died and she deserves it. Plus, I really like Coach Sawyer, and I like Raina even more. And now, finally, my oldest friend and my newest will get to meet each other and I'll have a group of my own the way Ryan did. Mom told me Zola ended up putting Beck and Theo in a private school for a while to give them a fresh start after we left. When Zola caught her up on things, she told me that Beck transferred back when he started to take football seriously so he could play at Lincoln High since the coach there had a friend who taught at UC Davis. Between separate schools, Theo's dance schedule, and soccer, we haven't had a chance to be all together yet.

When we pull up to the cottage, a knot forms in my chest. Ryan loved this place. We all did. But Ryan looked like he was home here. I walk inside and the warm smell of the baked macaroni and cheese dish in my arms is replaced by something equally familiar. The comforting scent of dried pinewood and fresh lake water swirls around me and though it's far too bright, I open my eyes as wide as possible letting the sunlight flood in through the wall of glass that makes up the backside of the modest cottage. The windows are open and I can hear birds singing their songs outside.

"Hello?" I call out. Footsteps thump from my right, and before I know it, Theo is wrapping her arms around my neck and I lean into her, careful not to drop the dish clutched in my hands. Zola appears a moment later, relieving me of my food carrying duties.

"Hi sweetie, it's so good to see you. Does your mom need help?" She asks, dropping a swift kiss on my cheek before gliding back to the kitchen to set the food on the counter.

"I'm just heading back to check."

"Don't bother. You just go get settled in. Beck! Come and help Emily, please!" Zola shouts down the short hallway. "How in the world is this still warm after the drive? You must spill all your mom's secrets." Zola says it conspiratorially but the comment puts me on edge, as if Zola is in on something and I'm not sure what.

I'm saved from replying when, a moment later Beck appears, pulling a Lincoln High hoodie over his head. "Hey Hart." He flashes a smile as he moves past me and out the front door. I walk slowly over to the sliding back door and step out onto the deck. Theo trails behind me telling me how Zola agreed to let her transfer back to Lincoln Middle School next year if she wants to, which of course she does. I nearly squeal and her voice fades away as I look out into the yard. Across the way, where the lawn meets the sandy beach, I see the dock. It's shorter than I remember. Then again, I was just a kid the last time I was here. Everything seems bigger when you're small. To my right is the tire swing the boys used to dare each other to jump off of when it swung out over the drop off.

I glance back at the cottage which looks cozy, and lived in. Dad used to come here too and I kind of wish he was still here. But I know mom always felt like he didn't belong. I overheard her one summer telling Annalee that she likes it better when he has to work and it's just the moms and us. She said he felt like just another mouth to feed and she was the only one with a husband tagging along since Annalee never remarried after her divorce from Tristan's dad and Zola would never give up her single life—her words. Theo loops one arm through mine, snapping me back from my thoughts, and I ask without looking at her, "Do you guys still come here a lot?"

Theo pauses and I wonder if she's deciding how much she'll tell me. "We do. But it's never been quite the same. It feels weird to come here with only us, and with Charlie being so closed off . . . then again, when we would come here with Annalee and Tristan, it was even more noticeable that you guys weren't here. It's just . . . yeah, not the same."

I nod, understanding what she means and wondering what we've missed out on. What Ryan has missed out on. Theo perks up. "But this is going to be great. You're here now and I'm excited to meet Raina."

"You're going to love her. And she'll love you," I tell her, smiling. "Hey, is Charlie here?"

Theo nods. "He's in the boys' room, reading. He said he needed a few minutes to settle in."

It's only ten o'clock in the morning, but it's already getting uncomfortably hot. It shouldn't be this hot in October but I guess Mother Nature does what she wants, so we walk down to the dock to dip our toes in the water while we wait for everyone else to make the near two-hour drive and settle in.

A few hours pass before I text message Raina to ask when she'll be here. She doesn't answer but just a beat later comes a knock at the front door. I jump up. "I got it!" I yell as I race no one to get to the front door first and swing it open to find Raina and Coach on the porch. I might have squealed while dragging Raina inside but lucky for me, she is just as giddy so I don't have to pretend to be cool about how excited I am. Theo appears behind me and I do a rapid-fire intro before Coach Sawyer cuts in.

He leans forward, purposefully inserting himself into our cluster like he's reminding us that he's also here. "Hey, Harley."

"Oh! Hey, Coach. Sorry. Good to see you. Mom's inside." He chuckles and I turn to see Mom walking towards us.

"Harley, at least let them get inside the door first." I roll my eyes. I don't mean to but I swear it's a reflex at this point. Raina pulls me to the side and Mom steps up to Coach. This is the point where I look away. I don't mind that they're dating but that doesn't mean that I need to watch them make out.

My back is turned but I hear Coach lower his voice, apologizing for something that I can't quite hear. I'm about to brush it off but Raina is staring at her dad and my mom with a weird look that I can't decipher, like she's waiting to see what's going to happen next. My mom's voice rings out. "Oh, of course, it's fine. The more the merrier." She sounds chipper but I've heard it enough times to know when she's faking it. When I turn around, I hear my mom at the same moment I see him. "Hi, Jeremey. I'm glad you could make it. Come on in and I'll introduce you to everyone."

He breezes past me. "Hey, Hart." He winks at me, sending the temperature in the entryway plummeting.

I follow our new arrivals cautiously into the living room where the sounds of happy chatter and boisterous laughter fill the cottage. A million scenarios flash before my eyes and I can't put a pin in any one reaction that makes the most sense. The one response I didn't anticipate was the absolute silence that envelops the room when Coach, Raina, and Jeremey follow my mom inside. The Moms look at each of us in turn, curious looks on their faces as they try to figure out what's wrong with us kids. Coach breaks the silence first.

"Hi everyone, I'm Sawyer and this is my daughter, Raina, and my nephew, Jeremey."

Zola rushes forward to take his hand. "We are so happy you could make it today. It's so good to finally meet you," she says, eyes flickering back and forth between Raina and Jeremey.

My knees feel weak, and I grow more anxious by the second waiting to see what Jeremey will do. He casts a quick glance in my direction before straightening his posture and painting a wide smile on his face. "It's good to meet you all. Thank you for having me." Jeremey sounds almost sincere.

One by one the conversations resume but it doesn't escape me that the moms are watching us. Are we acting funny? I feel like they think we're acting funny. I try to break the weird vibe by telling Raina and Jeremey that I'll show them around.

Slowly, everyone falls into a more comfortable rhythm and dinner goes off without a hitch. Jeremey is totally polite, asking for seconds of most dishes, even the twelve-hour salad that you eat at your own risk, which Zola can't get enough of. It's essentially mayo with a little bit of lettuce but she says Thanksgiving just isn't Thanksgiving without her grannie's salad. Even Coach seems to notice the sudden change in Jeremey. He doesn't say anything, no doubt not wanting to rock the boat. Jeremey asks after everyone, soaking in the tales of how we all came to be, while politely answering any probing questions from the moms. It's unnerving to say the least.

At only one point in the evening does it look like things might take a rocky turn. From the beginning, Charlie never quite settled in. I don't blame him. You can't look at anything in this place without remembering Ryan. A moment when he collapsed on the floor in laughter after swearing it was an accident that he spilled his water in your lap. A time when Ryan nearly knocked the table over from standing up too quickly to help wash the dishes with Zola. An occasion where he slipped your prized possession back in your hand when no one was looking because he couldn't bear to take it from you when he won whatever stupid dare was being doled out. And now Jeremey shows up out of the blue.

Charlie is staring at Jeremey with a blank look on his face. Totally undecipherable.

"Everything alright there, Charlie?" Jeremey asks calmly.

Charlie's face turns bright red and he presses his lips shut before pushing away from the table and walking off to his room without a word. Zola looks horrified, likely interpreting Charlie's upset as jealousy, or perhaps even anger at what looks like a new boy coming slipping into Ryan's vacant seat at the family table. I'm only guessing.

"Jeremey, I am so sorry. Charlie hasn't been himself. I swear he isn't usually like this…" Zola scrambles to explain but Jeremey cuts her off with a raised hand.

"Don't worry about it. No offense taken. Really."

I'm stunned. But conversation eventually resumes and Zola slips off to check on Charlie before returning to inform us that he simply wasn't feeling well.

My mom has been unusually quiet tonight, even though Coach is here. She makes conversation and every now and then I catch her and Coach looking at each other with those big glossy eyes, like they wish we all weren't here. But most of the time, she's watching Jeremey. I know she doesn't like him and she's warned me to keep my distance, but she still hasn't come out and said why. Something in her eyes tonight is different. Cautious. Like he's a wild animal she's afraid will spook if it hears the leaves crunch beneath her boots.

After dinner, Raina and I help clear the table while the grown-

THE TURN

ups sit outside talking, and the boys, minus Charlie, went down to the dock. From the picture window above the kitchen sink, I watch as they walk back toward the cottage, seemingly enjoying each other's company. Once the dishes are done, I leave to use the restroom, but before I get to the door, I hear low voices from the bedroom across the hall.

"It was you, right? I know it was." The voice is quiet, a little hard to identify, but it sounds like Tristan.

"Look, I don't know what you think—"

"Cut the shit." Tristan hisses. "What in the hell do you think you're doing?"

"I wasn't trying to hurt anyone. I just wanted her to leave."

My ear moves closer to the crack in the door so I can listen better. "You're playing with fire, and you know it. You're going to ruin everything." A pause, my brain scrambles to make sense of the conversation I'm hearing. "You know exactly what's at stake here. Back off and let me handle it."

"Relax, bro. It was just a little paint. Don't get your panties twisted."

"Emily can't find out."

I take one step closer, trip over a bubble in the carpet, and go crashing to the floor. The door swings open above me and before I can move, Tristan is hauling me to my feet and into the room where he closes the door. "Damn it, Hart! You were listening?"

My hands scrape down the front of my jeans. "I wasn't trying to but you were basically asking for the whole house to overhear, dummy."

Beck stands quietly off to the side. Jeremey pins me in place with a fiery stare. "What did you hear, exactly, Hart?"

"Nothing much." I lie, ready to slip out the door, but with

Tristan blocking my path, there's nowhere to go until they move out of the way. Jeremey just waits and it feels like a challenge. One I'm not going to back down from this time, no matter what he's capable of. "I know it was you." I spit the words through gritted teeth.

"You know *what* was me?" He pushes back.

"I know it was you that painted *murderer* on our front door, trying to scare us away from town."

I catch the confused look that Tristan casts to Beck before turning back to me. "No, Hart . . . you—"

"How could you do that to me? To my mom? After knowing everything we've been through . . . That's low even for someone like y—"

"Hart!" Tristan interrupts. "Stop. You've got it wrong. You don't know what you're talking about. He couldn—" But Jeremey is the one who cuts him off this time.

"No, no. She's right. It was me." My eyes flick back and forth watching Jeremey and Tristan exchange pointed glances that I can't quite interpret. It feels like they're speaking a silent language and I'm missing the point. I'm about to yell at them both but Jeremey presses on. "But look, it doesn't even matter because here you both are, right?"

There's a little truth hidden beneath his point, but I'm not ready to concede. "Of course it matters. You've done enough damage and I won't let you hurt us any more than you already have." I step forward getting as close as I can before Beck moves to restrain me.

Jeremey just chuckles. "It's all good Beck." He steps around me and whispers in my ear. "You're still a kid. Stop trying to play a grown-up's game."

Rage sparks every nerve in my body. I put the pieces together about what my mom must be so scared of. The articles noting her theory that Ryan was pushed, her crazed reaction around Jeremey, how she watches him and he seems to taunt her back. The thing is, before all of this, Ryan had also asked us all to keep Jeremey a secret. It's all starting to make sense. Mom thinks Jeremey is dangerous, I think she's right. Maybe Ryan was going to break his promise, and he found out Jeremey was dangerous too. But I'm not afraid of him. I'm livid and I have to know what happened. So, I poke him to see what the bear might do. "What are you going to do about it? Push me in front of a car?"

His stupid smirk slips from his face and I know my words hit their mark. "Be careful, Hart. This can get so much worse." I think it was meant to sound like a threat, but something wobbled in his voice and it sounded far more like a plea. He doesn't seem to realize that it only confirms my thinking.

Jeremey walks out of the room and Tristan hangs his head. "You shouldn't have done that, Harley." I don't understand. I've never been able to understand, in all my time spent reading the testimonies, Jeremey's name never came up. The boys all pretended like he didn't exist. They never came to my mom's defense. I know Ryan asked them not to tell anyone about Jeremey, even I kept the secret. But they knew what Jeremey did, and I didn't. They must have because they were all there.

"I don't get it." I don't want to cry but I can't help it as everything boils over and a tear streaks down my cheek. "What does he have on you guys? It must be something important. How could you let him get away with what he did to Ryan? You had to have known. All along." Neither Beck nor Tristan answers me. "I thought you loved us. We were like family."

Beck wraps me in his arms. "Hart, we are. How could you think that? This has nothing to do with—"

I shove him away from me, leaving the room before I fall prey to his fake comfort. "I hate you both."

"Hart!" Tristan's words are the last thing I hear before I slam the bathroom door behind me and throw the lock.

35

EMILY
Saturday, October 9, 2021

The game today has my stomach tied in knots, though I'll never let Harley hear me say it. From what Sawyer has said, the opposing team is known for their aggression, with players who seem to be competing for the most red flags by the end of the season. Referees regularly have to stop play to chat with the coaches and warn them if they can't maintain civility on the field, they'll be forced to forfeit. Harley has played tough teams before, but this team sounds like they're out for blood more than goals. I made Sawyer promise me he'd make sure the girls stayed aware of their surroundings on the field, and that he'd remain diligent being vocal from the sideline. He always is, but he knows I'm on edge today. The air feels thick with apprehension.

Equally unhelpful is that Jeremey seems to have waved a white flag, and though I have a couple decades of life experience on him, I can't figure out what it means. Since that night at the cabin, he's been entirely cordial. No cutting words, no undermining attitude.

Nothing. He's been respectful to Sawyer from what I can see and while I still catch him with a challenging look in his eyes, he hasn't lashed out in a couple weeks which makes our interactions more pleasant, but my mission to get him to confess to his vicious crime even harder. How do I press into someone who is being so utterly obliging? This must be part of his strategy. But, I still have no physical proof he is who I believe he is, and worse still, no one to corroborate my testimony. If I'm right, then why didn't any of the other kids react to his coming to dinner? My gut tells me that I'm right, but what if I'm wrong? What if I'm chasing someone innocent? Troubled, but innocent. I'm starting to second guess myself. Until I can get through this block, I'm stuck here, playing this sick game with the monster I'm nearly certain is responsible for Ryan's death. It keeps smacking around a haunting dread deep inside my bones. I'm not sure how much longer I can do this.

Sawyer is the one bright spot I have in this whole thing. Reuniting with him felt like curling up on the couch under a sherpa throw blanket with your favorite movie. With him, everything else seems to melt into insignificant puddles. It also feels like walking a dangerous tightrope where I want to let go and jump, to forget about Jeremey and just move on, but I can't because with Sawyer comes Jeremey. So, I'm left spiraling down until something gives.

I force myself to push that aside and focus on the field in front of me where Sawyer stands huddled up with Harley, Raina, and three other players who are watching him draw out plays on his whiteboard. He gestures wildly to the opposite side of the field and I follow his arm to find the opposing team lined up in militant formation performing synchronized warm-up drills. I look up at the stands behind me. They're fuller than normal and I wonder how many of these people came expecting a bloodbath. The thought makes my stomach churn knowing my daughter is down there in the middle of this while people look on.

My eyes roam the crowd for a moment before returning to the field where I see Jeremey walking along the sidelines in the direction of Sawyer. I track his movement, feeling like a voyeur but unable to pull my attention away. As Jeremey approaches Sawyer, he holds something out and a glare reflects off his hand directly into my eyes before I realize it's only Sawyer's car keys. Sawyer takes them from him and Jeremey turns around, stepping up to where Harley is doing a series of up-downs and toe-taps on the ball. She stands up and Jeremey leans in close to her face while my heart seems to slow. His mouth moves but I'm in no position to guess what he's whispering to her. Harley doesn't say anything back but I watch her spine go rigid, if only for a moment, while the color drains from her face. She returns to her warm-up as soon as Jeremey leaves to make his way up the bleachers.

He waves to me and I put a hand up as he gestures to the open seat next to me. I give a curt nod thinking I'd rather have him close to me where I have a more intimate view of his games, and he makes his way down the row.

"Thanks," he says. "I figured it'd be strange if there was an open seat next to you and I purposefully sat somewhere else. Since we're trying to get along for my uncle's sake and all."

I ignore his attempt at small talk. "What were you saying to Harley down there?"

Jeremey shakes his head casually, fiddling with a poker chip in his hands, its gold lettering flashing each time he spins the chip between his fingers. "I just told her to break a leg."

I look at my daughter while the pit in my gut widens, threatening to swallow me. The one that feels less like nervous energy. Rather like a warning.

    The referee blows a sharp chirp on his whistle to call the teams to take the field and I hear the opposing coach bark out a loud "Mark!" It's clearly an order as the players on his team each point a stiff finger at the girl directly in front of them, each seeming to claim one of our own for themselves in a show of intimidation. Raina looks behind her at Harley and bursts out in hysterics until she catches her dad's eye and slowly returns to neutral, unthreatened by the other teams display of dominance. Even from my seat in the bleachers, I can see Raina's sneer as she levels her gaze at the girl in front of her. The referee's whistle sounds again and the game begins.

    Twenty minutes of game play have passed and our girls are down 2-1. While they are so far unscathed, it's been a brutal quarter and they look exhausted. The other team is more physical than we even expected and their coach is already hoarse from barking commands. The referees have their work cut out for them and have already issued four yellow cards as they sprint up and down the length of the field. One of the opposing strikers breaks away and though it's out of her jurisdiction, Raina chases her down the sideline. As Raina closes in on her, the striker throws an arm out nearly sending Raina to the ground. I can almost see the switch flip just before Raina lunges off her left leg, reaching her right leg out for the ball in a slide tackle. Though Raina strikes the ball first, she sends the opposing player flying across the grass and the ball careens over to the opposite team's bleachers. The referee halts the game and races over to Raina throwing a yellow card up in her face. Sawyer and Raina are enraged at the error and even Jeremey stands with righteous indignation.

    "Open your eyes, Ref!" Jeremey yells. "It's a clean play, do your job!" It's the first time I've ever seem Jeremey react at a game at all and I'm surprised, to say the least.

Sawyer is on the field having a heated discussion with the referee and tempers finally seem to relax as he moves back to the sideline shaking his head. He throws his arms out in resignation, as the penalty will not be reversed and the opposing team takes their free kick, resuming play. Some time goes by without any fouls being called and Jeremey resumes playing with his poker chip in silence.

I point at the trinket. "What's that you keep playing with?"

"Nothing." He spins the chip between his index finger and thumb. A sigh escapes his lips. "It belonged to my dad."

"J.P. Is that your dad's initials?" I ask, watching the gold foil letters flash by.

Jeremey shakes his head. "My dad is Elliot Hammond. He said J.P. is a guy he used to know a long time ago, I guess. I've never met any of his friends. Not sure he even has any. He lives pretty off the grid."

After what feels like forever, the referee lets out two sharp chirps of his whistle signaling the start of halftime and the girls slog off the field while I exhale a sigh of relief.

I pull my phone out to check my work emails briefly, avoiding any more conversation with Jeremey. I've already talked to him more than I'd have liked but my curiosity got the best of me and sometimes when I look at him, I think *he's still just a kid*. I slide my phone back into my bag and as I'm zipping the top closed, he speaks.

"I know you hate me, Emily. And that's fair, I've been an asshole. I want to apologize and maybe then we can start over." I stare at him, floored. When I don't reply, he seems to retreat from his defensive position. "For my uncle, you know?"

There's remorse in his voice but it's difficult to reconcile with the twisted way he's been poking at my wounds until just a couple weeks ago. Is it real, or is it the next level in this hideous maze I'm being forced to navigate? I'm very nearly tempted to agree, weary from the mental fortitude it's taken to remain vigilant and prove who Jeremey really is. But the image of his leg shooting out, sending Ryan sprawling beneath my tires is a stark and painful reminder of what he's capable of. A reminder of what I'm searching for.

He's waiting for me to say something, and I can feel the tension as my brows dip, leveling a vicious look aimed directly at him. "Sure. Let's stop this fucked up game. We can start over. Just as soon as you take responsibility for what you've done."

Jeremey has the nerve to look surprised. "Em, I don't know what you're talking about . . ."

"Yes, you do, you little shit," I throw my accusation in his face plainly. No more vague allusions. "You were there. *You* pushed my son into the road that night. Ryan is gone because of you."

I watch my blow land and Jeremey looks around as if checking to see if anyone overheard. "That's a fucked-up thing to say. Do you hear yourself? If it was me, then why are you the only person who seems to know that?"

His blow makes a small chink in my armor and once again, I start to doubt what I saw that night, wondering if the trauma has cocooned me inside a protective narrative too strong for me to break free of. It was five years ago. Jeremey would have been just twelve years old, and I'd never seen him before that night. The possibility that I've got the wrong person, that I've got the whole thing wrong, digs a hole into my brain, making a home there. I'm nearly ready to apologize, to try to be happy instead of whatever this murky existence is, when his knowing sneer the day we met flashing in my mind. Jeremey gives a sad shake of his head before whispering, "You lost your child, I get that. I lost someone important to me too. But I didn't do what you think I did." Before I can say anything, Jeremey stands, exiting the bleachers and walking in the direction of the parking lot.

The referee has whistled for the teams to take the field for the second half and before I can turn my thoughts over in my mind, the game has started.

A few minutes pass by and I look towards the parking lot searching for any sign of Jeremey. Raina's voice pulls me back to the field as I hear her scream Harley's name. My head whips to the middle of the field where Harley is on a breakaway up the sideline. She's focused on making it to the goal, so much so that she doesn't see the girl running straight towards her, poised to make the slide tackle that will stop the play. I scream for Harley to watch her left side but she can't hear me from where I'm standing.

I see it all play out in slow motion. The opposing player turns her body, ready to slide, her left knee bends as she throws her body to the ground, her right leg extended, but her cleats are up and they glance over the top of the ball, slamming into Harley's knee.

Harley collapses, screaming in agony as Sawyer sprints onto the field. I'm down the bleachers before I can even process what I just saw. When I make it onto the field, I dart past the players who've taken one knee, over to Harley, where I see her leg bent in an unnatural direction, blood pouring from the gashes in her skin.

"You did this!" I scream, pointing at Jeremey who has somehow manifested on the sideline. He has the nerve to looked shocked and he holds up his hands in mock surrender as if I'm the crazy one here. "It was you! You told her to break a leg just before the game and now look at her!"

Jeremey takes a step back away from us. "It's an expression. It means 'good luck'. Uncle Sawyer?" Jeremey is pleading with Sawyer to help him but I'm ready to tear him apart.

Sawyer steps forward, grabbing me by the arms. "Em, I know you're scared but Jeremey wasn't even on the field. This was just a horrible accident. Let's focus on Harley."

"No, you don't understand. Sawyer, I had my friend look into him and I don't think you realize just how dangerous he is. You don't know who you're dealing with. He—"

Sawyer releases me and puts a hand up to stop me. "Wait. You looked into him? What does that mean? You went behind my back to what? Tell me how horrible my nephew is? Or to point out how I can't handle him?"

"It's not like that. It's just that he—"

Another step away from me and Sawyer's other hand comes up. "Emily, just stop. Let's just focus on Harley right now."

My mind snaps back to the field where my daughter lays sobbing. Medics set her leg as best as they can before loading her onto the stretcher laying on the medic cart. I climb in, heart racing as they drive us out to the parking lot where an ambulance meets us. I look back, only once and see Sawyer crouched down, face in his hands, diminished in height from the distance. I climb into the back of the ambulance while they load my sobbing daughter into the back. My eyes look back once more to find Jeremey standing further down the field directly where Harley's eyes would have gone to as she made her break away. Jeremey waits there, watching us, and taunting me with his hands stuffed inside his pockets, as paramedics close the doors and we drive away.

36

EMILY

Nearly four hours later, I'm still in the waiting area of the UC Davis Children's emergency room. Once the doctors were able to run all of the tests and scans needed to assess Harley's injury, they prepped and wheeled her back for emergency surgery to reconstruct her knee. Among the many lacerations, she suffered a fractured tibia along with a torn ACL and meniscus. Children tend to begin the healing process quicker and since Harley is still growing, it was imperative that she have her knee repaired quickly so that it sets correctly. All of this is done in an effort to avoid any further surgery down the road. My hands won't stop shaking. Harley's wails of pain reverberate around inside my mind on an endless loop. My phone has been ringing nonstop but I can't bear to talk to anyone right now.

When Sawyer bursts through the doors, I stand to my feet and very nearly tumble to the ground, weak and lightheaded. Sawyer is there in an instant, his steadying arms around me as he whispers soothing words in my ear as tears stream down my face.

"You're here," I say.

"Of course I am. Where else would I be?" He replies.

"How did you know we were here?" I manage to choke out.

"The paramedics told me. I have to fill out an injury report and I had to talk to them to fill in some of the gaps. I got here as soon as I could."

"I'm sorry, Sawyer. I'm sorry about flying off the handle earlier. It was like a reflex or something."

"Jeremey is a lot, I know. I'm not blind to his attitude. And you were scared. We're good." Sawyer squeezes me a little tighter.

I shake my head. "No, there's more. Things you need to know. It's important."

"We can talk about that later, Em."

I bury my face in his shoulder. "I'm still scared, Sawyer." For Harley, and for my own sanity.

"I know." His hand runs softly down the length of my hair.

"What if she can't play anymore? Or something goes wrong in surgery?" I'm trying my best to be calm, but my voice waivers, betraying me.

Sawyer guides me back to the seat and lowers himself down on the bench next to me, returning his arm around my shoulders. "Everything is going to be okay. I'll help her rehabilitate until she's ready to play again. I don't know how long it will take but she's strong. And so are you."

My eyes fall and my voice is barely a whisper. "I'm not as strong as I look. I can't handle this, Sawyer."

"You are. Look at everything you've already made it through. Divorce. Murder accusations written across your door. You lost a child, for god's sake, Em." His mouth is so close to my ear, as if he thinks the words will seep inside me more easily. He draws his face back and looks me in the eyes. "You're a fighter."

Did I tell him that someone wrote on our door? How did he know that? The thought pokes at me and I shove it to the side. Harley probably told Raina. Truly it could be anyone with the way gossip spreads like a virus through a small town like Lincoln.

I collapse into his arms, resting my head on his shoulder and wait for the surgeon to come out to tell us Harley is alright. "Where is Raina?"

"I took her home. She's there with Jeremey, waiting for an update."

Nearly half an hour goes by before the surgeon appears, striding over to where we're huddled together. "Ms. Sutton?" I nod, standing up. "I'm Dr. Callaway. Harley is out of surgery."

"Yes! Is Harley alright?" The doctor holds up her hands, telling me to slow down.

Dr. Callaway nods. "She's doing well. The surgery was a success but I'm afraid she's got a long road ahead. I was able to repair the tears in the meniscus and ACL, set the fracture in her fibula but she's going to be completely immobile for the first several weeks. After that we can assess her for a walking brace. Around nine weeks after that, we'll want to see her for new scans. If everything looks good, we can talk about the rehab process."

A lot of information is being thrown at me and though I try my best to keep up, my eyes must glaze over because the doctor informs me that all of this will be included in the discharge paperwork. "In all likelihood, she'll recover just fine with time. But because of the nature of her injuries, we do need to discuss the possibility that a full recovery can take up to a year depending on how her body responds and how seriously she takes the rehabilitation process. If she returns to her sport, the risk of reinjury will be higher in her case."

Sawyer steps in. "When can we see her?"

"You can come back now. Harley is in recovery, though it may take some time for the anesthesia to wear off. And just so there are no surprises, her leg looks much worse than it is right now. But I don't want you to be concerned." Dr. Callaway leans in toward me. "I'm very happy with how her surgery went. I have every confidence that a year from now, it will be like nothing happened."

"Thank you, Doctor."

She nods at me before directing us to follow the nurse back to Harley's room. Sawyer slips a hand through mine like it's second nature and leads me to my daughter.

The sight of her takes my breath away. The tubes and wires are imposing, and her leg rests elevated on top of her hospital blanket, bruised beyond recognition. Deep, ugly gashes where the cleats ripped her skin have been stitched up and her knee is the size of a small watermelon. The doctor explains that they need to ensure there's no infection at the surgery site before Harley gets the hard cast that she'll wear while the bone heals. I send a silent prayer of thanks that she is unconscious right now as I spiral backward five years and the memories of both my children being stuffed into an ambulance intermingle, making it hard to know which memories are which. A feeling that I nearly lost Harley too consumes me and I throw myself into Sawyers chest, sobbing.

His arms are warm and he squeezes tighter, forming himself into a security blanket around my heaving body. "I'm sorry, Em. I am so incredibly sorry."

"For what? This isn't your fault."

He pulls back, eyes glistening. "I promised to be vigilant on the field. I knew what that team was capable of and I let my guard down. I should have warned Harley, but I was frozen." Sawyer hangs his head, sniffing. "I failed her. I failed you."

My heart breaks apart a little more. "You haven't failed either of us. You're here. And if you weren't, I'm not sure I'd be able to get through this." I wrap one hand gently around the back of his neck, tugging the bottom of his hair through my fingers, looking at him earnestly. "I'm so glad you're here," I whisper, angling my face up towards his. His lips are full and I know they'll provide a desperately needed distraction from the horror that is my daughter's leg lying on the bed across the room.

His body moves closer to mine and I feel his arms around my waist, gently stroking my lower back. Sawyer's eyes lock with mine. "I wouldn't be anywhere else right now."

I should have fought harder to stay away from him.

His lips float closer and my mouth opens, beckoning him near.

I should have reasoned with myself that I need time and space to figure out what's best for all of us.

We haven't kissed since our date but I've thought about it every day since.

I should stop this now before it goes on too long. This could end badly and it's not fair to Harley.

There was a moment at the cabin, but with so many people there we were constantly interrupted. It was probably for the best but with his arms around me now, I can't for the life of me recall one good reason why we shouldn't see what happens.

Circumstances aren't ideal but now that I know my daughter is safe, I find myself gravitating towards him. Towards a place where I'm safe too.

I close my eyes, relishing the moment our lips meet, relishing this moment that saves me from this room.

37

HARLEY

Opening my eyes is more work than I ever imagined. My body feels like it's hovering in the in-between, a weight drags it back down to Earth before something snips the cord sending it floating back into outer space. Mom is here. I can see her through the tiny slits my eyelids are able to form. I hear her apologizing for something but I can't hear what. Something about Jeremey?

I must have fallen asleep again. My eyes flutter open for just a minute. Just enough to see my mom again but she isn't talking now. And Coach is here too. They're . . . kissing. But not just kissing. Full blown making out. Ugh, gross. I wonder if this is what people mean when they talk about fever dreams, because while I've seen them make the eyes at each other and Raina told me they kissed, I've never seen them paw at each other like this. My parents weren't affectionate either, not that I can remember anyway. I want to stop thinking about my parents this way. Do I have a fever?

I'm so tired. My eyes snap closed again, though I'm not sure how long because the next time they open, my head feels clearer than before, but my mom and Coach are still groping each other. "I'm sure there's an empty room somewhere if you two would like to continue this somewhere private." I chuckle a bit when they startle apart, but it hurts too much when my leg starts to bounce. Mom swipes at her mouth, erasing any evidence of Coach. I wish it would wipe out my memory too. It's not that I don't want her to be happy. I really do. I just don't need to see it.

Especially right now.

Mom is at my bedside in a second. "Hart, how are you feeling?"

"Like a million bucks. Put me in, Coach." My throat feels like sandpaper and I don't recognize my own voice. I put off the only question that matters to me right now. I know a trip to the hospital and surgery means I'm not in good shape, but I just want another few moments before I find out exactly what my situation means. Coach Sawyer moves to the opposite side of my bed and hands me a cup of water. I take a sip from the straw before trying to talk again. "You know, it's supremely fu—effed up that I had to get sent to the hospital to get you two to admit how into each other you are." The googly eyes are back and if I'm not mistaken, Coach is actually blushing. They don't say anything though and when I look at my mom, her eyes have a glossy sheen to them, outer corners turned down. "How bad is it?" I squeeze my eyes shut, preparing for the blow.

My mom takes my hand. "Bad, honey. But—"

"How bad? Season ending? Career ending? Don't sugar coat it."

Mom takes a deep breath. "Season ending for sure but likely not career ending so long as you take your recovery seriously, do your rehab, and listen to the doctors. Don't push it and try to get back out there too quickly."

The tears I was trying to hold back leak out and my bottom lip begins to quiver. I'm wide awake now and the devastation is sharp. Coach steps forward. "I am so sorry, Harley. I should have called out to you. I saw that girl coming but I couldn't get the words out fast enough."

I sniffle. "It's not your fault. It's my job to be aware of the players around me. I was too focused on driving down the field."

"Harley, we are going to get you back out there next season. Alright? You have my word. I'll be right by you every step of the way."

I nod, staring down at the gnarled lump that used to be my knee while they tag team detailing my treatment plan. I'm not really listening. Images of a different outcome flood my brain and I replay my breakaway over and over, memorizing each piece. The length of the field until I reach the goal. The face of the player hovering over me as my bone basically sticks out from my leg, my blood oozing onto the grass. Not one, but two teammates were there, making themselves available for me to pass to. I should have passed the ball and cut outside of the defender in front of me. "Coach, do we play them again next year?"

His head flops forward and a full belly laugh bursts free. "Harley, one step at a time. How about you focus on getting out of here, and back to your home first? Then we can talk strategy for next year."

I roll my eyes but it only makes him laugh more. Next year, I'll be ready for them. This time next year, everything will be different.

38

EMILY
Tuesday, November 16, 2021

It's been nearly six weeks since Harley's accident and though it scares me to relax, Harley is thriving. So much more than I expected given her level of disappointment that day in the hospital when we told her she wouldn't be playing soccer for nearly a full year. Sawyer seemed equally shocked when I told him Harley came home and launched head-first into a highly organized recovery and rehab plan. She's made sure not to try walking before she's supposed to, and resting at the appropriate intervals after getting her blood flowing.

Harley is so close to being able to transfer into a walking boot and start physical therapy. Her spirits are high, reminding me so much of her brother who always strove to see the brighter side of life. I attribute much of Harley's optimism to Sawyer who has found ways to keep her close to the sport she loves most in this world. Harley is at his side during practices and games where he includes her in team strategy and play creation. He asks her what she sees on the field, which players need to be rotated or substituted, and where improvements can be made. She studies from the coach's side of the game and helps Sawyer devise practice drills. Once he's reviewed the statistics and game logs for the upcoming opponent, he passes the information to Harley and asks her what she thinks, comparing notes. Harley bounced back mentally in no time and we're already looking forward to seeing how this new angle translates onto the field next year.

Tonight is a team dinner that one of the other parents set up as team bonding and Harley insists on going even though she's still on crutches. Raina has promised to keep an eye on her and let me know if Harley needs to come home and rest. I can't deny her this moment of reprieve, and when Sawyer asked me to come to his house for dinner, I jumped at the chance since it will be the first time we've been alone with any modicum of privacy, and I have yet to see where he and Raina live.

The front door swings open and Sawyer's smile stretches all the way to his eyes. He grabs my hand and pulls me inside, swinging the door closed behind me. A hand reaches up, tenderly cupping the side of my face and he leans forward planting a sweet kiss on my lips, his other palm presses against the door behind my head. "Hi."

"Hi." My voice sounds breathy but I'm starting to grow accustomed to it. That's what Sawyer does to me. Steals the breath from my lungs and I feel an addiction beginning to take hold. I stopped needing anyone besides my daughter when Ryan died, so this urge feels risky. But, it's exactly that risk that makes me feel alive again.

Sawyer cranes his head down to graze his lips over my neck, not wasting any time. I can't recall a time I've ever felt this desired. My thoughts are interrupted and I silently curse myself. "Where did you say Jeremey was tonight?" Jeremey has been avoiding me, which is a welcome change. He's been visiting with his parents more often, staying with his dad when he can. The two weekends we've made it up to Zola's cottage, Jeremey opted to stay with his dad both occasions. I haven't let go of my duty to Ryan, but other things, like Harley's recovery, have taken priority and I'm trying to savor the peace while I have it.

"He's . . . with his . . . dad," Sawyer replies between kisses. He pulls back just enough that I can look into his eyes. "It's just you and me tonight."

My eyes flicker down to his mouth and I press my body into his. "Mmm, thank God."

Sawyer chuckles and scoops me up, wrapping my legs around his waist as he carries me to the couch where he lays me down reverently. His fingertips graze the back of my calf and he watches his own hand as he runs a slow touch up my thigh, pushing my dress up higher and higher, where he stops at my waist, teasing the hem of my dress. He looks at me, asking if this is alright. I nod and he grins as he falls into me. When he does, I let myself fall into him too.

I'm a puddled heap in Sawyer's lap, thirty minutes later, every limb jellied and satisfied. My head falls softly onto his shoulder while his arms wrap around me from behind. Sawyer lazily strokes a finger up and down my arm while I trace the tattoos on his arms with my eyes.

"Sometimes I can't believe you're here." Sawyer hums in my ear. "Seemed like everyone in town was talking about you coming back but I just didn't believe it until you walked into the arena that day."

I soak in the sweet timber of his words while he continues his tiny finger trails along my skin and I move a little closer, a tiny thought creeping into my mind threatens to pop the fragile bubble I'm floating in. A chill zips up the length of my back. "How did you know they were talking about me? You didn't know my last name was Sutton when Harley and I showed up that day."

Sawyer pauses. "I have a secret I've been keeping, Em." The temperature in the room plumets, despite my proximity to the warmth radiating from Sawyer's body. "I ask around about all my clients." He chuckles softly. "One simple question to Mrs. Nedley and woman couldn't shut up about you."

I swap Sawyer playfully on the shoulder. "You're shameless." He cranes his head and nuzzles his face into my neck making me laugh involuntarily. When he finally relents, I ask, "So then, you already knew about Ryan?"

He nods. "I knew that you lost your son some years ago." His free hand glides up to stroke my cheek. "I figured you'd tell me when you were ready." It's my turn to nod. "Or when my asshole nephew decided it was time. Whichever came first." A laugh bursts from my chest but the mention of his name takes me out of the cocoon we've made. I don't want to be thinking about Jeremey right now. I want to forget. It feels so good to forget, just for a moment.

My clothes are on the floor next to the couch and I drag myself from my lusty little bubble and pull the layers back onto my body. Sawyer pulls his T-shirt over his head and I sneakily watch the muscles in his back ripple as the fabric slides down over his skin. I could have stayed in our bubble for days, I'm sure, but when Sawyer asks if I'm hungry, my stomach betrays me, gurgling at an embarrassingly loud volume.

"Where's your bathroom? I'm just going to go freshen up." I

THE TURN

throw an arm out in the direction of the hallway, assuming it's the right direction.

Sawyer grabs my hand and pulls the back of it to his lips. "Second door on the right," he says. When he pulls away, his hand holds mine until he physically can't reach any longer. I wait, watching him turn the corner into the kitchen before I move towards the hall.

39

EMILY

As I wander down the hallway toward the bathroom, I slow to a stroll and look at the photos that hang on the walls. Moments in time, frozen into memories. There are classic school photos of Raina over the years next to an artistic still of Raina taking a shot during a soccer game, her leg extended and the ball tracing a perfect arch through the sky. One photo shows a close-up of Raina sitting on her dad's shoulders, arms wrapped around his forehead as if she's holding on for dear life. Sawyer's eyelids are pulled back by her fingertips and his mouth is open wide in what looks like a boisterous laugh. I smile as I wonder who took the photo. Who was there to capture such a perfect moment? I pause for a just a moment more before continuing down the hall.

A step further, to my left, is what must be Raina's room. The door is open so I steal a peek inside. The bed is unmade and there are articles of clothing littering the floor. Her walls are decorated with posters of Megan Rapinoe, Crystal Dunn, and Alex Morgan.

THE TURN

On top of her dresser and shelves are trophies and an assortment of medals, mixed with bottles of nail polish, headbands, and a few books. I take a step back and turn to continue down the hallway to the find the restroom.

Across from Raina's room is another bedroom. A quick glance shows that it's neat and orderly. The color of the bedding and drapes are a dark, navy blue. An interesting contrast to the room I just caught a glimpse of. I'm about to move on when something on the nightstand catches my eye. It's the only item out of place on a surface that is otherwise fairly tidy. My curiosity gets the better of me, and I glance over my shoulder and listen to make sure Sawyer is still cooking. When I hear the clinking sounds of the pans against the stovetop, I step inside to get a closer look.

There, standing up next to the small bedside lamp, is a tiny Lego figurine. The Hulk. I run a gentle finger over the tiny action hero. There must be tens of thousands of these exact figures in existence, but the sight of him is so painfully familiar that a wave of years old memories comes crashing into me, the ones I went searching for in Ryan's room all those months ago. I blink them back and sift through the stack of papers sitting neatly on the tabletop.

The paper on top shows an essay with a huge red "F" written on the front with Sawyer's signature scribbled on it and a pair of black reading glasses sitting on top of it next to a pair of gold pilot's wings. Beneath it is an old travel magazine. Under that, the corner of a photograph peeks out and my pulse begins to race. Can Sawyer hear it from the kitchen? The pounding is deafening. The image of an old tire swing looks back at me as sweat begins to form on my upper lip. I wipe it away before putting my index finger on the picture and sliding it slowly out from under the stack. My breath catches in my throat as the rest of the photo is revealed.

It serves me right for snooping around where I don't belong. I shouldn't be in this room. But then, neither should this.

Why does he have a photo of my son? Why does he have *this* photo of my son? I search the furthest corners of my mind for a reason, any reason, that could explain how this picture found its way into this bedroom.

What should be a stranger's bedroom, if everything he's told me is to be believed. But he's been keeping more secrets. I look around the room for anything else that might soothe my thoughts and make the connection I need to understand. But I come up empty handed.

I should have kept walking, but how could I?

The temperature in the room plummets and the photo gripped between my fingers begins to shake as my hand trembles. A clanging sound from the kitchen reminds me that I'm not alone in the house, and I wasn't given permission to cross the threshold into the bedroom.

"Emily?" His voice calls for me. I know he's just down the hallway, preparing dinner, but he sounds much further.

"Be right there! Just washing my hands!" I shout. I quickly decide that I have a minute, maybe two, to look a little closer before he'll come looking for me. I slide open the drawer on the nightstand and rummage through the junk. I sift through crumpled packs of cigarettes, half eaten bags of candy, and a condom. Nothing to explain what I found. I'm about to plunge my hand back into the drawer when a voice sounds, suddenly right behind me, startling me so badly that it's all I can do to hold onto the photo now hidden behind my back.

"Can I help you find something?" His voice is cool, not a hint of emotion buried underneath.

It sparks every instinct within me telling me to leave. Now.

40

EMILY

"Jeremey, hi." I scramble for any reason as to why I am digging around in what must be his bedroom. Though he's the one who owes an explanation. "I was just looking for the bathroom." Lame, I know. But I'm not sure anything I might have said could make this less unnerving.

Jeremey watches me, his arms crossed at his chest and waits. He cocks his head to the side and his eyes float down to his bedside table. "And did you find the bathroom in my nightstand?"

I need to try to diffuse the situation before it gets back to Sawyer. "I'm sorry, Jeremey. I didn't think you would be here."

"You know what? You're right. I wasn't supposed to be here." He winds up, and I can tell he's ready to fight. "Should I go then? So you can feel better about looking through my stuff?"

Asshole.

I hold his eye contact while the hand behind my back slowly eases the photo into my back pocket. "No. No, I'll just go. Sawyer is waiting for me." I make my way to the door but Jeremey doesn't move to let me pass. I shift sideways to slip past him and he turns his head to watch me go. The bathroom is to the right, further down the hallway, but I go left and hurry back to the kitchen.

Sawyer is scooping risotto onto two dinner plates when he notices me hovering by the table. "There you are. I thought I'd lost you." He grins at me and continues to put food onto our plates.

I force a smile while I find my composure. "I just wanted to clean up a bit."

Footsteps echo behind me and Sawyer looks over my shoulder. "Jeremey! What are you doing here? I thought you were with your dad tonight."

I brace myself for the accusation that I know Jeremey is ready to throw Sawyer's way. He wouldn't be wrong, but it's still a discussion I can't have right now. Not with the hole burning through my back pocket. I could interrupt, make my excuses, and tell Sawyer I'm not feeling well. Maybe that could explain my riffling through Jeremey's room.

"I came back early. Dad called and said he had to fly out for work. Last minute. Shocker." Jeremey shrugs, as if his dad leaves him hanging often. "He said maybe this weekend if he's back."

Sawyer's smile falters. "I'm sorry, Jere. I know you were looking forward to spending the weekend with him."

Jeremey shakes his head. "I wasn't really." He doesn't elaborate further.

I watch as Sawyer tries to lighten the mood. He holds out a plate. "Would you like to join us for dinner? There's plenty. I'll fix you a plate." Sawyer turns to pull another plate down from the cabinet.

"Don't worry about it. I'm just going to hang out in my room. I have some homework to do." I think about the failed essay sitting on his nightstand.

    Sawyer starts to insist he join us but Jeremey is already gone. And I'm left here, trying to pretend like everything is normal for an entire meal, wondering if Jeremey is going to tell Sawyer about my rifling.

41

JEREMEY

Emily isn't nearly as slick as she thinks she is. It couldn't have been more obvious that she swiped the picture I planted. I'm not in it and that just made it so much better to watch her squirm, trying to figure out why I have it. I wonder exactly how stupid Emily must think I am. Dumb enough to leave this stuff laying around, out in the open, purely by accident? Good. That's just perfect. Let her think that. She ruined my life and she still has no idea what she did to me. And it's starting to *really* piss me off.

42

EMILY
Friday, November 19, 2021

Unease pools in my gut while I navigate the beautiful, twisted, narrow roads to Zola's cabin. Harley has asked me several times if I'm alright and I try my best to hide my thoughts from her. One of the side effects of it being just the two of us for so long is she can see right through me. She must have her own things milling about in her mind because she leaves me be and we drive quietly for some time.

I weigh the consideration of asking Harley about the picture. Prying a little more to see if she has any explanation for why Jeremey might have this photo. I'd be keeping my word to be more open and honest with her, but it would also require me to confess to both how I found it in the first place, and to the fear making its home in my chest. The one telling me I underestimated how dangerous Jeremey is.

The cabin is just up ahead. I've run out time. I missed my chance. Or have I been saved from being forced to unravel the snarls in my mind a little while longer?

Twigs snap and pinecones crunch beneath our tires as we pull onto the driveway. The forest is serene and when I cut the engine, the melodic sound of bird chatter float all around us. I make the decision to turn and face Harley just as she darts out of the car, nearly running up the porch which is exactly what her new walking boot is not for. Relief, or perhaps frustration, rushes through my veins and I grab our bags from the trunk of the car and cart them inside to settle in. The cottages are laid out so that there is plenty of space between homes. Enough privacy that your neighbors aren't watching your every movement, but not so much that you feel isolated from the community. Inside, everyone has already arrived and settled in. Zola and Annalee are in the kitchen prepping dinner while the scent of cinnamon and vanilla with hints of orange seep from the oven, filling the room.

"I made my grandmother's orange cinnamon rolls," Annalee explains. I tell her how delicious they sound. They really do. I ask if there's any coffee left over from the morning and Annalee shakes her head. "I'll put some on. I could use a cup myself. I'm wiped out!"

We catch up for a few minutes and I summon as much calm as I can. Harley went straight to the back room where Theo was waiting for her. "Where are the boys?"

Zola returns the pasta she's just drained in the colander to its pot before answering. "I think Tristan and Beck are in the boys' room playing video games or something. Charlie is at his grandma's." My head droops. "He just wasn't up to the visit. Friendsgiving was just too much for him and he thought it'd be best if he hung back."

"I'm so sorry to hear that. I thought he was doing better?"

"He was. Is. But then, he's been away from everything all this time. Shoving him back into everything without so much as a warm-up was hard on him."

Annalee calls Tristan to the kitchen to open a jar of olives for her. He breezes by calling out a greeting of sorts to me on his way back to Beck. That was weird. Annalee just rolls her eyes, looking at me. "Boys." She says it simply, a universal truth that everyone understands. Only I don't, understand, that is. My boy wasn't able to turn seventeen. It's not Annalee's fault I'm spiraling though. I push my lips into a sort of smile and stare out the window.

It's nearly dusk and my head is throbbing. Another extra cup of coffee probably isn't the smartest idea but what can I say? Coffee consumption is absolutely one of my red flags. My head is already swimming enough to keep me up all night no matter if my eyelids do weigh a metric ton. Might as well sharpen my focus so I can think more clearly. I step out onto the porch with my mug and stare out at the lake. This space that holds so many precious memories for us over the years. A place well documented through photos like the one I found in Jeremey's room.

How do I talk to Sawyer about something I don't fully understand? Sawyer will want to jump in feet first and grill Jeremey but that won't solve anything. It won't ease the fear blooming in my gut that I misunderstood Jeremey's behavior towards me all this time. At one point, his actions could have bene chalked up to a stupid, but fatal, mistake made by a child. But his behavior over the months paints a different, crimson-colored picture. I underestimated how dangerous he is. Besides, what exactly does that picture prove? It's circumstantial at best. Who's to say how he got it or why he has it? But the image of the tiny Lego tugs at a nagging thread in the back of my mind. A thread that might unravel everything if I pull too hard. Am I ready for that?

I walk a few steps out onto the lawn that leads to the lake, pausing to take a sip from my mug. A breeze nips at the hairs on the back of my neck, making them stand on end and that's when I feel it. The heat growing as a pair of eyes burn into the back of me. My body whips around and there he is.

Jeremey.

Standing on the back porch of the neighboring cottage.

Watching me.

The sun casts an eerie light from behind him but when I squint, I'm sure it's him. I turn back to the house, ready to march over there but I'm frozen as I see Tristan on the porch looking to where Jeremey stands and then back at me.

When I look back to the porch next door, Jeremey is gone. I turn back to Tristan. "You saw him too, didn't you?"

Tristan only shrugs. "Saw who?" He doesn't wait for my response before turning to go back inside. When he moves, I see Harley for one fleeting moment. She'd been tucked behind Tristan but when she saw me, she dashed inside ahead him.

The pair of them are being dodgy, even for them, but I'll deal with that later. I race inside, slipping my tennis shoes on before marching next door to find out exactly what's going on.

43

EMILY

Manners are second nature at this point, but they fade quickly when Jeremey doesn't answer my polite knocks or the ringing of the doorbell. It isn't long before I resort to pounding on the door, yelling his name. "Jeremey! Open the door! I know you're in there, I saw you watching me from the porch!" I wait a minute. Nothing. "Jeremey!" I lean to the side to look through the windows that line the door. The house looks vacant. There is minimal furniture and a painting or two, but the place is otherwise empty. I begin walking around the cottage to peer inside each available window, but it all amounts to the same conclusion. It doesn't look like anyone is here at the moment. No shoes on the floor, no clothing thrown over the back of the couch. No dishes left out on a table or in the sink. I press an ear to the back door, listening for noises coming from inside before all common sense vacates my mind and I attempt to slide the door open. It doesn't budge, saving me from myself.

Returning to the front porch once more, I realize there's no car in parked out front and looking at the dirt, I don't see any tire tracks either. My brain has been a mess, sure, but I'm nowhere near full blown hallucinations of Jeremey standing on a porch just thirty yards away from me.

I peek through the other windows but from here, it's dark, the surrounding trees block what's left of the low hanging sun. Rays peek through the branches vying for space, obscuring my sight and hindering me from getting a clear view of what's happening inside the cottage.

Flashes of dusky sunlight through the trees from six years earlier cut through my vision, intermingling with what's in front of me and my heart begins to race.

I slide my cell phone from my back pocket and bring up Sawyer's number. He answers on the third ring. "Hey, Em. Miss me already?"

"Is Jeremey with you?"

"I . . . what?"

"Jeremey. Is he there at your place right now?"

"No, he's not. Em, is everything alright? You sound a little anxious."

"Where is he? Do you know?" My pulse swells inside my throat threatening to burst through my skin as the view before me begins to tunnel.

Sawyer clicks his tongue. "What is going on? Why are you so concerned about Jeremey all of the sudden? I thought you were at Zola's place."

Forcing myself to slow down, I inhale before responding. "I'm sorry. Look, I will explain everything when I get back into town. But I really need to know where Jeremey is right now."

"He left early this morning to stay with his dad."

I file this new information away, trying to remember if I know where that is.

"Remind me, where did you say his dad lives exactly?"

"Well," Sawyer starts, "he has a little place up North. I'm not sure where, exactly. I've never been there."

"Is there any way you can find out for me?"

Sawyer sighs. "Let me text his mom. But, Em, you better start explaining soon. You're starting to worry me."

I wait. "I'm sorry, Sawyer. I really will explain everything. I can't explain right now because I'm not sure I understand what's happening myself." The longest minute ever passes before his cell phone chimes, the noise floating through the receiver.

"Okay, let's see. Landry says his dad has a small cabin on—" His voice cuts out.

"Sawyer?"

"—On Lake Harding. Em . . ."

"I'll call you back." I disconnect the call before Sawyer can say anything else and I race back to Zola's.

44

EMILY

Tristan and Beck are sitting on the back porch watching me. Harley is on the front porch and I'm tempted to go straight for her but just before I'm about to yell out for Harley's name, I catch the boys exchange a quick glance with each other so I change tactics and march over to them.

Beck moves to go inside. "Freeze, Beck. You and Tristan just sit down. We need to talk." I'm huffing and exhausted by the time I make it up the few steps to the back porch, but I chalk it up to the worry currently making my chest expand. "You saw the boy on the porch, didn't you?" I ask them, either of them. I couldn't care less which one wants to confess first.

There it is again. That same knowing glance flickers from Tristan to Beck. So quick you'd miss it if you didn't understand how teenagers communicate when they think they've been busted. But despite how long we've spent apart, I do know these boys. "I saw that. Beck, start talking. His name is Jeremey, right? And you boys know him. From before." I'm not asking anymore.

I watch his Adam's apple bob up and down before choking out a small "Yes."

I sit down across from him and look him right in the eye. "Who is he?"

Beck shoots an invisible apology to Tristan before talking. "He's no one. Just a neighborhood kid."

"Which neighborhood? This one? Because I've never seen him around here until just now."

Tristan twists in his seat. "This one . . . and Lincoln. He's been around. But he's just some kid who used to ride bikes with us sometimes. Alright? That's all!"

I look back and forth between the boys, searching for something that will tell me what I already know to be true. "How is it possible that he came to ride bikes with you and I never knew about him?"

"I don't know, okay? I don't remember. His dad wasn't around much because he was a pilot, and sometimes he'd fly out of Lincoln. Jeremey was always by himself and he just found us one day, recognizing us from up here. That's all I remember." Tristan crosses his arms defiantly across his chest like he's twelve again. I look at Beck and see silent tears have begun streaming down his face.

"You know why I'm asking about him, right? He pushed Ryan into the road that day." Beck's tears fall faster and his chin begins to quiver. "You saw him do it. Why didn't you guys say anything?"

Beck explodes. "No! I'm not doing this again. We did what we had to. And I can't go back there. I won't!" He storms into the house and Tristan takes off behind him. I wonder if I pushed too hard, too fast. I don't want to break them, not again. But it's not about them right now. This is about Ryan, and how long I've waited for justice. I've waited long enough.

45

HARLEY

Mom comes barreling around from the back side of the cabin, calling for me. I was trying to listen to her phone call once I saw her practically breaking into the cottage next door, but she whipped around before I could get back inside. I was going to go lock myself in my room with Theo but then I heard her going at it with the boys. She has a crazed look on her face and I can see that this is it. I feel it. I swore never to tell, but something changed just before we drove up here. She looks spooked and I know I'm going to have to explain some things.

"Harley!" I stay where I'm at and straighten my posture. Mom is always griping about the way I slouch, telling me better posture makes a stronger core which of course will help my game. I googled it after her millionth reminder and damn it, she was right. "Harley, we need to talk."

"About?"

"You've been watching me pound on the neighbor's door so

I'm guessing you have at least a vague idea, yeah?"

My eyes fall to the ground. "I have an idea. There's something I need to grab before we talk."

"Alright. I'll go sit on the dock. Come sit with me once you do." Mom walks off and a moment later, I'm in Theo's room sliding a photo album from her shelf. I don't need to check the contents, I know this album well and I fold my arms neatly across the cover, pressing it to my chest as I hobble my way to the dock.

What's left of the light bounces off the water, shining spotlights up onto the shoreline. I watch as my mom brings a hand up to her brow. I lower myself slowly to the empty space on the planks beside her and pass her the photo album. She doesn't say anything while she flips through the pages.

"Harley, I don't understand. Why am I looking at this?"

I think carefully about how I was to respond. This feels like a situation where I should get something in return. "We're going to trust each other right now, right? We're going to be honest with each other?" My bottom lip starts to tremble.

Mom wraps an arm around my shoulder. "Of course, Harley. What's going on?"

"I mean it." I choke out the words between sniffles. "Because if I tell you the truth right now, it feels a lot like betraying Ryan. So, I need you to tell me the truth back."

"Alright." Her grip on my shoulders tightens. "I hear you."

I gulp down a steadying breath. "I swore an oath never to tell."

"Never to tell what?"

My brain feels scrambled and I'm not sure where to start, so I reach across her to pinch the cover between my fingers, gently pulling it back to reveal the first photo. "I know Jeremey. Err, knew him."

Waiting for this to sink in feels like an eternity. "I don't understand. What am I looking at, Harley?"

I try to swallow the lump forming in my throat. This is it. The moment I'll be free of this secret I've been living with. "Jeremey was one of our summer friends growing up. He's always been around."

Mom's eyes are like glass and I can see the wheels turning behind them. "I'm trying here, honey, but I'm not following. You've all known him. All this time. But how is it that this is the first I'm hearing of this? Why isn't he in any of these photos?"

The photo in her hands begins to collapse, crinkling under the pressure of her grip. "That's what I'm trying to tell you, Mom." I gently peel the picture from her grasp. "He is. Look." I point to the background, just there under the tire swing. A figure, hidden in the shadow next to the tree trunk. Anyone would assume it was just some person wanting to try out the tire swing. Mom flips to the next photo, scanning it carefully, finding the scraps of evidence of a bystander nearby. Then the next one. A stray foot peeking out from the neighboring porch. The back of a head looking out at the lake. He was always so careful to stay away from the camera lens.

Finally, she pauses. "You're telling me that all of these people are Jeremey?" I nod. "How? Next door. Those were just renters next door."

"That's what I'm telling you. They weren't. It's just that Jeremey's dad wasn't around much. You guys assumed and so you didn't bother to get to know them. And we didn't tell you."

She pulls out the photo that each of us kids has a framed copy of. "This one. He's not in this one, but I found this in his room the other night." She says it like it proves something, though I'm not sure what.

"Jeremey is the one who took that photo. It was our last summer together here." I shrug, not knowing what else to say about it.

My mom chews on the inside of her cheek, while tiny creases form in her brow. "How could you guys have kept this from me? From all of us?"

"Jeremey made us swear never to talk about him. He told us that his parents had problems and that they fought constantly. Said they used him as leverage against each other. Sometimes—a lot of time—he was left there at the cabin alone to fend for himself. He was scared that if anyone found out, they would call child services and he would get taken away." I take a deep breath before continuing. "I never really liked him. He always seemed to be starting little fights between the boys. But Ryan said he needed a friend and that we could be that for him. Ryan made us promise to keep Jeremey's secret. I'm so sorry, Mom."

She's staring at the remaining pictures clutched in her hand and a finger trails over Ryan's face. While I feel the weight of the secret lifting, the guilt grows heavier. "What happened after that summer? Did you guys see Jeremey when we weren't here?"

I shake my head. "That was the last time I saw Jeremey. You know Ryan didn't always let me tag along when we were home so I'm not sure if he ever did. Once I heard Ryan and Charlie arguing about Jeremey. I don't remember ever knowing why." I chuckle slightly at the memory. "I got really good at eavesdropping."

That gets a snort out of Mom. "Oh, I remember. You still are." She shoots a snarky look at me. "Harley, has Jeremey said anything to you about Ryan? About his accident?"

"No, but that's why I'm telling you this now. I know you hate him and that you're worried about me when he's around. And you said Ryan was pushed by a kid you didn't know, in the court transcripts." I place the pieces at her feet, showing her that I've put them together. But I want her to say it. I want her to hold up her end of the bargain.

She doesn't answer to that and I feel my temper rise. She promised me the truth in return. "What has he been saying to you when you guys are alone after games?"

I cock my head to the side. "He's been reminding me of the mess I'd make by telling you all of the things I just did. How I'd be betraying Ryan and . . ."

"And what? Harley! Betraying Ryan and what? And who?"

"That's all!" Mom doesn't reply and my frustration boils over. "Mom! Why won't you tell me what you're getting at? Say it! I was honest with you. Your turn."

"Do you remember that Sawyer said Jeremey started causing trouble around six years ago after he lost his best friend in a car accident?" I nod. "I think that friend was Ryan." She pinches her lips between her teeth like she doesn't want her thoughts to escape her mouth. "And yes, I believe Jeremey is the one who kicked Ryan into the road."

My mouth hangs open and my mind goes blank. I can't find a single thought to grab onto. "Are . . . are you sure?"

A small nod is all she gives me and she seems to resign herself to explain further. She might as well. This isn't the sort of accusation you come back from. "It's a massive risk for me to throw out an accusation like this without proof. I have to be careful. I need the boys in my corner because, at the end of the day, Jeremey is a juvenile and we are talking about a six-year-old crime. If they backed me up, I might have some legs to stand on, but I have no real evidence. There is none. Nothing to tie him to it at this point, outside of eyewitnesses and that doesn't buy much since they have already testified to the exact opposite before. But I'm sure." Mom takes a breath. "He's been taunting me since he showed up at that first lesson. After everything you just told me, and what I found in his room, it makes perfect sense. I can see it so clearly in my mind now."

"Are you sure you aren't just seeing what you want to see because you don't like him?" This is more than I ever thought she'd tell me and I'm not quite sure how to feel about it. I knew about Jeremey and I kept that secret, for Ryan. But I wasn't there the day he died and everyone did their best to keep me out of it. I don't think my mom is crazy for believing someone pushed Ryan. I think it's what she honestly believes. But does that make her right?

Something in Mom snaps and I'm completely unprepared for the eruption. "Of course I don't like him! He murdered my son, damn it! And now he's set his sights on you, threatening you, scaring you! Look at what he's already done to you, Harley! Your leg . . ." A tear slips from my eyes and she pulls back. "Oh, Harley, I'm so sorry, honey. I . . . I . . . " Her arms are around me in an instant and I choke down a sob.

"It's fine. I'm fine, Mom."

"It's not fine. But, honey, listen to me. You did the right thing telling me. And now, I need you to tell me something else." A breeze nips at my neck sending a shiver down my back. "Earlier, you saw him here. You saw him on the porch over there." It isn't a question, but I answer anyway, nodding my head. As afraid as I am of what might happen if Jeremey finds out I betrayed our summer pact and turned him over to my mom, I'm far more afraid of what might happen to my mom if she thinks I'm still choosing Jeremey over her. Over us.

Mom gives me a firm nod and stands abruptly, turning towards the cabin next door. She's ready to go to war, but as it turns out, the war is already here.

"Hey, Hart. Emily." Jeremey's voice is like silk, sliding over to us from where he stands at the end of the dock.

46

JEREMEY

I expected at least a bit of surprise from the pair of them and the lack of reaction is a letdown. Emily looks ready to take a swing at me. Or maybe worse. Her eyes bore into me while she tells Harley to go inside. I take a step back, giving Harley some space to hobble past me.

I've barely looked up when Emily barrels toward me. "I know it was you," she seethes.

"What's that now?" This feels like a good time to stop testing her and play dumb.

"Harley told me everything. I know you used to mess with my kids all summer long and I know it was you." Her finger is a sharp needle in the soft spot on my shoulder, but I don't so much as wince. I won't give her the satisfaction.

"You've got me all wrong, Em."

"Don't fuck with me you little shit. I know exactly who you are and I'm going to prove it."

I shove my hands into my pockets and take one step back. "What exactly is it that I'm supposed to have done?" She's said it before but I want to hear it again. I want to know exactly what she's thinking. It's precisely what I want her to be thinking.

Her tongue pushes against the inside of her cheek forming a little lump beneath the skin. "You killed Ryan. You pushed him into the road that night, six years ago, and he died. You're a murderer and you've been threatening Harley, Tristan, Beck, and Charlie for years to keep your hideous secret."

She lunges forward and I teeter on the edge of the dock trying not to fall into the shallows behind me. "Emily, really. You have no idea what you're talking about. I didn't push Ryan."

"Don't lie to me!" Her hand lashes across my face, lighting my cheek on fire before I've even realized what just happened. But it's alright. I've endured a lot worse for a lot longer.

"You still don't remember me, do you?" Emily, to her credit, doesn't flinch. "Oh, this is going to be good." A tiny twitch in her upper lip. "You and I go way back, Em." Another quiver. "You ruined my life that night when you called the cops on me." And another wobble. Each one better than the last.

"More lies. This game is tired already. Why don't we just let the police sort out your story?"

"You mean the way they sorted it out before? Yes, they did a stellar job."

Emily takes a step closer to me. "I was just a kid. And all I wanted was a friend. My parents made it so damn hard to keep any. You saw me looking through the window, watching all these kids here but instead of letting me come inside, you sent the cops after me. You took one look at me and decided I wasn't good enough for your precious family. Because of you, my parents were so furious that I was barely allowed out of the house ever again. Just a pawn in their custody games. You ruined my life!"

Her face goes slack, the realization visible across her eyes. I can see the moment her memory sets in. "You . . . I thought you were looking for a way in. You were a stranger and I was afraid you were going to steal something, or hurt one of my kids."

"I was ten!"

Emily's eyes narrow at me and a switch flips. "I was protecting my family. I wasn't such a bad judge of your character as it turns out. I won't let you hurt any of us anymore."

I turn my face to the house, finding Tristan focused on us from the back porch. The sight of him seems to snap some sense into Emily, who's going to have to figure out how to explain to Tristan what he just witnessed. I turn back to Emily and smile. "You can hate me all you want. I couldn't care less what you think about me. You can't prove shit! You couldn't before, and you sure as hell can't now."

My chest thumps where she shoves a photo into it and storms off calling after Tristan.

I peel the photo from my shirt, taking in the smiling faces staring back at me. Harley, Theo, Tristan, Beck, Charlie, and Ryan. I feel the sting of angry tears filling my eyes. The same tears I never allow. Sometimes I wish I'd never gotten involved with any of them. When Ryan died, I lost the only friend I had that ever really cared about me. But I can't bring myself to regret it. I did what I had to because he deserved it. No one else would look out for him the way I did.

The wind rustles the edges of the photo and I bite back the tears before I release the picture, letting it fly away, landing softly on the glossy surface below me.

47

EMILY

The cottage feels empty when I walk through the sliding door. "Tristan!" I call out. His shoes are silent as he steps out from the darkened hallway. "Where is everyone?"

He draws aimless shapes on the floor with the toe of his shoe. "Harley was upset about something earlier. They all went for a walk, I guess." I wait to see if there's any more explanation. "Mom was going to come get you but Harley said not to. She left a note on the counter." He jerks his head towards the kitchen.

Tristan looks more anxious than I've ever seen him and tears fill my eyes. I blink them back and sit down on the couch, sneaking a glance outside as I do. Jeremey is gone and I return my focus to Tristan, patting the seat next to me on the couch. "Sit with me."

He scuffles over to the couch and eases himself onto the cushion beside me.

"We were always close, weren't we? You know that you can talk to me about anything, right?" His only response is a sad nod.

"Is there anything you'd like to talk about? Something you've been carrying around, wanting to get off your chest." Tristan sniffles, but shakes his head. I pause for a moment. This is the boy who used to paint me pictures each summer. The same boy who taught me how to draw a cat using only three shapes. He's nearly an adult, but sitting next to me, he's huddled into himself like a child afraid of some inevitable consequence coming to him. "Aren't you tired, Tristan? Haven't you carried this around long enough?"

A tiny chunk in his armor becomes a crack. "I'm so sorry, Emily." He sniffs again. "I didn't want to. I was just trying to protect you."

"Protect me from what, Tristan?"

"From all of this! I didn't want you to come back and have to relive everything that happened to Ryan. It was bad enough the first time. I thought if I could just scare you away then I could save you from having to run away again." His face falls to his hands.

"Tristan, what? What are you talking about?"

"The paint on your door. It was me. I know Jeremey probably told you. I'm sorry! Mr. Candor told Mom that you were back when she went to the farmer's market in June, so I rode over to your house one morning and waited until I saw you leave. I didn't mean to hurt you or Harley. You know I would never do that." Tristan swipes the back of his arm across his nose.

"Oh, Tristan." He has no idea what Jeremey told me. He took a shot but he missed. I wish I had time to be gentle about it, but I don't. Too much time has passed already. "Tristan, I don't care about the paint. You've been lying about something else. Something so much bigger." I reach into my back pocket and pull out the couple of photos I still have on me, placing the tiny stack into his hands. I point at Jeremey in the background. Tristan's eyes are as wide as two golf balls and they whip up to meet mine. "I know the truth, Tristan. It always comes out eventually."

Tears slip from his eyes and he starts to cry, dropping his head to my shoulders. I wrap my arms around him instinctively. It's a special sort of heartbreak to hold a mournful seventeen-year-old boy you've known since he was a small child. "It was an accident. He didn't mean to," Tristan chokes out between sobs. "We had to protect him."

"Tristan, what he did was a crime. A horrible crime. He has to be brought to justice. For Ryan."

"No! You don't—understand. W-w-we couldn't t-t-tell—anyone. We couldn't do that to him. Not after everything he'd been through. We couldn't." Tristan's shoulders start to shake and his words are choppy and strangled.

I softly stroke the back of his head trying to calm him so that he can speak. "Honey, listen. I know that he had a hard time with his parents growing up. Harley told me he was alone a lot and he told you he'd get taken away. But that doesn't mean he doesn't have to take responsibility for what he did to Ryan. He killed him, Tristan!"

"I miss Ryan so much. I thought about telling so many times." Tristan's voice is barely a whisper and I have to angle my ear down to hear better. "But I just didn't want to have to miss another one of my best friends too. I don't think he even realized what he'd done at first. Even weeks later though, months even, he just kept saying he didn't feel right without Ryan here and I just couldn't. I couldn't do that to him. Telling someone would have meant losing him too and taking him back there all over again."

A flicker of something sparks in my mind. What is it? It's close but I can't quite grab onto it. I push Tristan's shoulder back so that he has to sit up and look at me. "What did you say?"

His face is soaked with tears and he gazes at me through swollen eyes. "I don't think he really understood what he'd done at first. He was standing next to us, but he wasn't there, you know?"

"No, after that?"

He thinks for a moment. "He kept saying he didn't feel right without Ryan here?"

Memories unravel in my mind, sending me back through the last few months, where suddenly, I understand. I see it all again with painful clarity.

"Tristan, I have to go. I'll be back as soon as I can. Will you be alright?" He nods and I text Zola and Annalee to tell them I'll be back when I can. The door bursts open as I pick up my keys and Beck slogs inside, followed in quick succession by Zola, Annalee, Theo, and Harley.

She must have seen the blaze lighting my eyes, because Zola doesn't hesitate. "Em, is everything alright? Where are you going?"

"Did you know?" I pinch my lips together and wait.

"Know what?" Zola's confusion sounds genuine. "Em?"

"Did you know it was him? Did you know?"

Zola's hands go up in surrender. "Em, I have no idea who you're talking about or what they did."

My eyes find Harley's automatically. She looks afraid and I hate it. Her glance darts to Annalee standing in front of her. "I told her about Jeremey. I think that's who she means." Harley's voice is barely a whisper. "Mom, I'm sorry."

Annalee looks to Zola. "Jeremey? The kid from dinner?" Zola shrugs and I barrel past them. I can't handle going through this again. Not right now.

When I get to Harley, I pause. "Harley, it's alright. I promise. I have to go somewhere. I need you to stay here until I get back.

Alright?" Harley nods, looking like the little girl I cling to in my mind. I kiss her on the cheek and I can hear Annalee realizing Tristan is in distress as I shut the front door behind me.

48

EMILY

The door feels fragile beneath my knuckles and I suck in a breath to steady my fist. A moment turns into a lifetime as I wait. The door creaks open just a bit and I steal myself as I watch a mask of shock slide over the face before me.

"Emily? My God. Emily, what are you doing here? Are you alright?"

I give a curt nod. "Is he here?"

The confusion morphs first into understanding, and then into surrender. Eyes drop to the floor as the door opens further, revealing him seated on the couch, staring out the picture window in front of him.

I step inside, slowly, moving closer. I am woefully unprepared for this conversation. I still have no real proof, though Charlie's reaction to my arrival seems evidence enough. My heart already aches at the thought of losing another boy who has already endured so much. And it wasn't his fault. Not really. "Hi, Charlie."

His gaze slowly makes its way to mine and it's apparent that he's been crying and I wonder if one of the other boys, Tristan probably, called him. I turn back to his grandmother to thank her for letting me in and then I sit beside him, wrapping him in my arms. I expected to fly into a fit of rage when I saw him. All this time—years, in fact—he's kept this secret from me. They all have. But when I look at him, the only thing I see is a tortured soul. A little boy in so much pain, so deeply buried in grief that he hasn't been able to return to us. My rage dissipates instantly and all I have left is sorrow. For Ryan, and for myself. And for Charlie.

A minute passes, maybe more, and I sit back to look at him. "I know, Charlie. I know what happened." I scrape my thumb beneath his eyes, pushing the tears to the sides. "What I don't understand, is why?"

The Adam's apple in his throat bobs once, twice, and his mouth opens. "It was an accident. I didn't see the car coming." I can't tell if he's being kind by not mentioning that it was my car specifically, but I don't correct him. "Jeremey was just trying to protect me. They all were. I'm not going to say I'm sorry, Emily. I can't. Sorry isn't enough and if I say it, you'll either say you forgive me, or you'll hate me forever. I can't stomach either."

A tiny piece of my heart chips away as my hand reaches up and pushes a piece of his hair away from his face. "What happened, Charlie?"

His shoes fidget with the carpet and he picks at the nail on his thumb. "I loved Ryan. He was my best friend in the whole world. But . . ." Charlie trails off. "But sometimes it felt like he didn't really see me. He didn't understand me. But then Jeremey showed up one day. Made us promise never to tell anyone about him because he'd get taken away from his family. His family was broken, like mine. He was broken like me." Charlie sniffles. "He didn't have any friends and he told us his parents didn't want him and bounced him back and forth." Charlie rakes his shirt sleeve across his upper lip and his eyes fall to the floor. "Sometimes, it was hard being around you and Annalee and Zola. It reminded me of what I was missing and I'd just get so angry. I just wanted to not be there, around it all, you know? Ryan, Beck, and, Tristan didn't let me fade into the background, but I really wanted to sometimes because otherwise it just hurt too much. For the first time, it felt like someone saw me. Jeremey got me . . . and, I don't know. Maybe since he didn't have many friends, he didn't have any expectations for what being a friend looked like. He let me just be when I needed that and I guess we sort of bonded. I don't think Ryan liked it."

Charlie looks up at me as if gauging my reaction to that. "It's alright, Charlie. Keep going."

"Ryan was always good to me. And we agreed to keep Jeremey's secret. But I guess sometimes, it just felt like he was jealous or something. He'd make little digs at Jeremey, saying it was all in good fun. We started arguing more but I just figured it was regular guy stuff. I just thought friends fight sometimes. In a weird way, it felt kind of good. Like I was finally just a normal kid. Does that make sense?"

I nod. It's a sad thought but I understand.

"Anyway, the fights got worse. Or not worse. More frequent. It felt so out of character for Ryan. It's not really fair, but I guess I understood why he'd feel like he needed to take jabs at Jeremey. Jeremey always stuck up for me, always encouraged me. But then Ryan started taking little pokes at me too and Jeremey always snapped back, defending me." Charlie's gaze pulls away from me once more. "I tried to just ride it out. I tried to man up like my dad told me to. But . . . I don't know."

I drop an arm around his shoulders. I want him to purge this from his mind. For himself, and for me. I need to know that I wasn't crazy that night. "But what, Charlie? What happened?"

He runs a hand down his face and sighs. "We were riding our bikes that day. Tristan and Beck were up ahead a little way. Ryan was next to me and Jeremey was just behind me. They were arguing about who beat who in arm wrestling earlier that day. Ryan said Jeremey cheated because he lifted his elbow off the table, and Jeremey told him to quit crying like a little girl and take the loss. I tried to make peace like I always do but Ryan kind of turned on me. He accused me of always taking Jeremey's side over his and that made me a bad friend."

Charlie digs at a piece of skin on the side of his thumb and blood begins to pool at the surface of a tiny tear he made. He starts to cry again and the rest comes out chopped in pieces. "I tried . . . to explain . . . but he . . . he . . ." He sniffs loudly pulling a strand of snot back into one nostril. "He was so angry . . . he told me if I was so in love with Jeremey, I should take him home to meet my mom . . ."

My heart splinters at this confession. Instinct begs me to defend Ryan, to tell Charlie he didn't mean it, that Ryan was a nice boy. Rationally, I know that people say hurtful things, even when they don't mean to. That my son could say something like to this Charlie, knowing what he's been through is a devastation I'm unprepared for.

Another smear of mucus paints the sleeve of his shirt as he scrapes it along his nose before continuing. "I think he must have realized what he'd said because he looked sorry, but I can't be sure because everything started to get a little hazy. I saw Jeremey pull around in front of me, yelling at Ryan for being an asshole because he knew my mom was dead and I just . . . I just . . . snapped. I guess my foot flew out and I kicked him hard enough to knock him into the street. I didn't even know I'd done it until I heard the screech of the tires and someone screamed. Maybe it was me. The next thing I knew an ambulance was there loading Ryan into the back and Beck and Tristan were yelling about Jeremey and telling me what the story was. It was all happening so fast. Jeremey made them swear never to tell any of it before he bolted. He said if they did, he'd make sure the families knew they'd been lying all along and that they covered up Ryan's death. He said it would rip us apart. I was so confused and scared and . . . oh God, Emily, I killed him! I killed my best friend! I didn't mean to!"

That's the last thing Charlie says. Tiny, unintelligible sounds are all that escape his lips for the rest of the day. We sit there for a long while, me on one side, Charlie's grandma on the other and just held him until he sobbed himself to sleep. I look at him and anger bubbles but I swallow it each time, too exhausted to determine whether it's at Charlie or at the world. And I can't bear to be so angry at Charlie. Not after everything he just told me. I lay him down on the couch and drop a blanket over his shoulders before his grandmother and I go into the kitchen.

She wastes no time. "What are you going to do with that, Emily? It was a horrible, horrible accident. And now you know." She pours sweet tea into a cup that she thrusts at me. "So now the question is, what are you going to do?"

I stare down into the tea, watching the tiny ripples disappear as my tear drops into my glass. My head shakes before my thoughts can catch up. Seems my subconscious can process everything I just learned a lot faster than the rest of me. "Nothing." I purse my lips. "Now, I let go so I can be at peace. I know exactly what ripped us apart." I sigh. "So . . . I'm going to make sure Charlie gets the help he needs. I can't lose him too." I look her in the eye, filling my chest with resolve. "And I'm going to figure out how to be happy. I think Ryan would want that."

Charlie's grandma crosses the kitchen and pulls me into a deep hug, warm with gratitude. She doesn't say anything for a long time and when she pulls away, we simply look at each other.

"I've got to get back to Harley, now." I reach for a notepad and pen I see sitting on the Formica next to us and I scratch out my cell number. "Will you call me when he wakes up and tell me how he's doing? I'm going to work on finding him a new therapist. Zola had said a while ago that he seemed to be at an impasse. I think he could use a new therapist, given everything he's been through."

"Of course," she says, pressing a hand to my shoulder.

I take one last look at him, my son's closest childhood friend and I whisper, "It's not goodbye. It's see you later." The sound of the door latching behind me feels final, but I make a promise right there, to myself and to Charlie, that I won't let it be. I'm not running anymore.

EPILOGUE

CHARLIE
One year later . . .

It had been years since I'd ridden a bicycle and now the wind in my hair feels like freedom. I've been riding it a lot lately as part of my therapy. Emily stuck close by me since the day she came out to Truckee and she found me a new therapist who came highly recommended, Dr. Glover. Or Hannah as she insists I call her. Hannah thought it was time that I reclaim some of my childhood experiences that were taken from me, like riding a bike.

I started riding to Emily's house regularly to have dinner with her and Harley since I've moved back in with Zola. Sometimes my grandma would join and then I'd go back to Truckee with her when I needed some space. Things are getting pretty serious between Emily and Sawyer. And Harley is crushing it on the field this season. She worked hard to rehabilitate her knee over the last year and it's paying off. They seem happy and I'm glad because they deserve it.

A couple months after Emily's visit, after I purged the shame and guilt from inside me, the truth came shooting back up to the surface and I realized I wasn't the one who kicked him over. It was Jeremey.

Everything was a blur when I saw Ryan fall into the road, but later on things slowly started to crystalize.

With Harley and Emily returning, it was impossible to ignore the day Ryan died. I couldn't escape what happened. It played on an endless loop in my brain. Hannah forced me to face it all head-on, and helped me evaluate what really happened that day. I picked the scene apart, frame by painful frame, and then put the pieces back together, stepping back to find that it revealed a whole new picture.

Jeremey lied to me.

He'd always been a liar, always pitting us against each other. But this was different. This was unforgivable. Jeremey took my best friend away from me. From all of us. After everything Ryan did for him, to bring him into our group and stick up for him, Jeremey saw an opportunity to pin his death on me. Poor little broken Charlie. So, when he calmly explained to me and Tristan and Beck what happened, how I'd snapped but Ryan was being a dick, I bought it. I believed him. Besides, he was right about one thing. There was no proof. It was our word against his and he was an invisible boy we'd all kept hidden. How could we explain that? Besides, by then Jeremey had disappeared. Everyone did, really. Emily and Hart were gone. Ryan wasn't here. I still had Theo, Beck, and Tristan but it was never the same and they all wanted to just move on.

But throughout my recent therapy, I realized that Emily was right too. Ryan's killer needed to be brought to justice. Hannah taught me that I need to start focusing on gratitude because it will start to shift the way I see the world. So, I'm grateful that I unknowingly lied to Emily last year because that leaves me free to bring Jeremey to justice.

I've been riding around long enough. I'm ready. Everyone is at Zola's cabin preparing for dinner. Everyone but Jeremey. When I asked Jeremey what he was up to this weekend, he had apparently told Sawyer that he'd be visiting his mom. But I know him better than that. Even after all this time. I ride in from the far side so that no one at Zola's sees me and I park my bike against the side of cottage.

A sliver of me still wars over what I know I'm about to do. After all, Jeremey is still someone's child. Someone's nephew. This will hurt innocent people. But Hannah said that karma is always at work, so this is simply Jeremey's karma coming back around. I ignore the part that tells me karma will come for me too. Then again, what can karma really do to hurt me after what I've been through? Emily lived through the loss of a child. Landry will too. Besides, at least in Landry's case, she'll still have hope because her son will go missing. Hope keeps people around, keeps people moving forward, so I'll give her that gift. I'll make sure of it.

I knock on the door, looking around to make sure I'm still alone. He's taking his time and I wonder if he knows what's coming or if this is just his way to make sure he's never caught lurking. I move to the right and look through the window where I catch a peek of him and toss him small wave. He walks towards me and then, the door swings open. "Charlie," he says, looking past me. "What are you doing here?"

"Hey, Jere. Can I come in?"

He nods, moving aside and closes the door behind me.

ACKNOWLEDGEMENTS

This book, third in the trilogy, was by far the most challenging yet. I could reflect on all the many reasons I suspect that was the case, but that's not what these pages are for. Though I must say, as hard as it was to get to The End, the hardest task was yet to come. I'll try not to let my fear of leaving someone out consume me. So, here we go . . .

While much of my time is spent alone, working through the pages before these, writing is not the solo endeavor most think it to be. It is a constant communication with the reader as we carefully craft what we want to tell them next. It is a constant collaboration with those who inspire and improve upon its foundation along the way. Without any of the following people, this book would not exist.

To Amanda, my editor and sounding board. Stephen King put forth two notions that you've proven to be true. (1) The editor is always right. And (2), to write is human, but to edit is divine. Thank you for slogging through the trenches of this manuscript with me, for countless coffee-drinking work dates, and for taking your red pen and keen eye to this story time and time again to make it divine.

To every book club who selected one of my books to read and discuss with your friends, thank you.

To the IBPA for inviting me to speak at the IBPS Publishing University and connect with readers, writers, and publishers from all over the country while honing my craft, thank you.

To Sam Schlafer and the Lincoln Library for inviting me to speak at the first annual Book Festival. It's an honor and a privilege to collaborate with you. Cheers to many more successful festivals in years to come.

To Brood Coffee for letting me practically move in while I hammered away on my keyboard over the last year, and for continued support of our local community, thank you.

To Old Town Pizza, Rebel Hen, Bayabelle, Fowler Ranch, and the town of Lincoln, California, thank you. I love our little town. Places like yours that serve others with that small town joy and community passion, are exactly the kinds of places that make me never want to leave.

To Kane Brown for putting on one of the best concerts I've been to this past year, and creating songs that cut to the heart of some of these characters and helped me focus on what matters most.

To every new friend, author, reader, publisher, librarian, bookstagrammer, booktoker, supporter, family member, podcaster, conference and festival worker, bookstore owner, photographer, graphic designer that I've met along the way, thank you. You make this journey truly special. It's not for everyone, but because of each of you, it's one hundred percent for me.

To Hailey, Frank, and Raegan (who finally understand what it is that I do), you and your father remind me why I write, and provide me with all the very best reasons not to do it all the time. To my other Frank who has never given me any reason to think that I can't do this, thank you. I love you all immeasurably.

ABOUT THE AUTHOR

MARISSA VANSKIKE is the author of *How It Had To Be* and the award-winning thriller, *Bronswood*. When she isn't busy shuttling her children to their various activities, you can find her outside with her family or caffeinating herself with a book in her hand. She resides in Northern California.

For more content, or to connect with the author, please visit:

www.marissavanskike.com
Instagram: @marissavanskike

THIS BOOK INCLUDES CONTENT AND MENTIONS, EITHER ON OR OFF THE PAGE, OF THE FOLLOWING, WHICH CAN BE TRIGGERING:

Blackmail
Car accident
Murder and attempted murder
Death of a child
Death of a sibling
Death of a friend
Post traumatic stress disorder
Child abandonment
Bullying
Gaslighting

www.ingramcontent.com/pod-product-compliance
Ingram Content Group UK Ltd.
Pitfield, Milton Keynes, MK11 3LW, UK
UKHW031259060225
4478UKWH00030B/373